LIVING
IN A
THUNDERSTORM

A Fictional Story
By

Matthew Wride

Edited by Emma Wride

First Published 2021 by

ISBN: 978-1-80049-975-1

"See, to live is to suffer. But to survive. Well, that's to find meaning in the suffering"

EARL SIMMONS

X

For Alex, Teagan & Joe xxx

Prologue

This overdose got me sliding up my living room wall it's in my blood I can't stop it but I will not fall the turning point and I'm sick of this shit the voices pushed me but I didn't wanna hear it

For the last 17 months I'd turned so many corners I'd become dizzy. I was still an alcoholic but I had a purpose in my life. I.Had.A.Purpose.To.Live.

I was named Tennyson after a poet, so it felt appropriate to name my dog after my favourite poet too. I had my fucking dog. I had Kano. I hated the world and everyone in it but I loved that little dog. He never judged me or left me when I fucked up, like everyone else had. In my deepest darkest times, that little dog pulled my through. He was my friend, my only friend.

Mentally I'd been getting better, I could feel it. Dev, Ref and Gel, the three voices in my head, had stopped talking to me so much. I thought I'd miss them if they left me, but now I had Kano, he was my salvation from the darkness of the mental abyss I was staring into. My reason to get up in the morning and drag my drunk ass to work. My reason to give the world a second chance.

I'd not indulged in a single barroom brawl in over a year as I could feel an anger had been lifted from me. However, two thieves had tried to snatch Kano from the garden last summer and experienced how my love was actually a lot more vicious than my anger. I left tread marks on both their faces, to the point I had to bin my trainers incase the shitbags decided to press charges. They never did. They got off lucky. If they would have tried that shit with John the biker or gay Tony, who both lived on my street, they'd be fucking dead on the pavement.

Kano had given me the loyalty I'd always craved, and I would have killed anyone who hurt my best friend.

After an all-day drinking session I blacked out in the house and I left my front door ajar for the best thing I've ever had and the only thing I dared to care about since Genevieve left me my boy left me he fucking broke my heart but in the end it was me who killed my dog I.Killed.My.Dog.

I'm sorry boy I didn't mean to fuck up again I can't help it I'm ill I didn't want you to leave me that's not why I left the door open I love you boy I'm made for the misery I didn't deserve you but I'll see you soon I'll see you again really soon boy I.Will.See.You.Soon.

It's 10 PM on Sunday night, I'm sipping my beer and whiskey rather than swig it as normal as the shops don't open until Monday morning. To stop me finishing my booze too soon I have been popping a 30ml Dihydrocodeine every 3rd song as I make my way through Outkast's first 3 classic albums (Kano's favourites). As I take the ATLiens CD out and replace it with Aquemini, I feel totally smacked out. From the research I've done, 90 to 120 ml was supposed to get me a nice mellow and smacky high, which it probably would have done if I'd let the 120 kick in first. The 15 pills I was given to help with a medical condition were now dissolving in my alcohol filled belly. Each fresh tablet lying on top of the previous one, on top of the previous one, on top of the almost dissolved previous one.

My body broke down the pills, the pills broke down my mind, my mind buried my soul. I was fucked up but I was happy. I think. I sat slouched on the sofa. My whiskey glass empty again.

As the southern jazz of Outkast's beats filled the room I felt an invisible presence push me against the wall. Both shoulders flush against the cold wall my body starts to lift me towards the ceiling but my feet don't move from the floor. Pinned to the ceiling and looking down at my lifeless body; I loved the way my living room looked from this angle with my Air Max still both planted firmly on the floor with both feet in them. Was this an outer body experience or was I just high as fuck? The high became a low as I floated back down into the lifeless tattooed vessel. I was 37 years old and I was a chronic alcoholic. I was not suicidal, but a suicide through drinking or drugging myself to death I saw as nothing more than the inevitable end to an unfulfilled story. I just wanted to see my dog again.

Death didn't take me that night but it did leave me fucked up with some good rib shots thrown in. My internal organs never functioned properly again after this OD and the pain still bothers me years later. I was still high as hell the next morning while walking to the call centre, bouncing up the road like I was walking on the moon. I was constipated for the next 3 days and just sat on the toilet blasting endless, loud, empty farts with no substance. Sort of like the customers who called me on a daily basis, time wasters, FUCK OFF!

Every ship has to sail stormy seas and I'd been in the storm for 25 years. I'd tried to drink myself to death on numerous occasions many times, and failed each time. My time would come.
I'm.On.My.Way.Boy.

February 28th 2018

Chapter 1

1835 days served in the Royal Navy with well over 1500 of them either mildly intoxicated or completely shitfaced. Dozens of days in police cells and interview rooms, both military and civilian police were not fans of the drunken Welsh chef. I'd travelled the world and caused chaos and carnage wherever I roamed. From the hidden whore houses of Alexandria where our suspect Egyptian taxi driver dropped us, to the seedy and sweaty New York City streets in a hot July. I was young, single and paid.

I joined the Navy as a handsome 21-year-old boxer with enough capabilities to have had a half decent record in the pros. I left at 26 years old, alcoholic and out of shape. A vicious temper egged on by years of alcohol abuse. As a boxer I was washed up. As a Chef I was shit. And as for relationships? I was a dog. I made a decision that my future didn't lie on the waves so I handed my notice in. One year later, I left. Honorable discharge, time served. I headed home to Swansea, a place 6 years previously I had left to escape a life of violence, drugs and petty crime. I was back.

Still single and with no children I definitely knew about, it was time for another fresh start. I did receive a letter to the ship three years previous from a lady called Tanya. I spent the weekend with Tanya when the ship was conducting sea trials off the coast of Norway. She was tall, slim and blond with a pretty face. Even though I never found out her age I would have said she was at least 10 years older than me (and she fucked like a demon). Tanya claimed I had fathered a child with her, a daughter. The letter didn't specify anything in particular that Tanya wanted from me and I was not told the child's name or sent a photo. I threw the letter away and didn't write back. Tanya never contacted me again.

I had 2 months of holiday pay and long service at sea pay to keep me good for the next few months. I also had a half decent place to rent that would give me a good base to go into the second half of my 20s a bit more tactfully than I did the first half but little did I know what was ahead. After being out of the Royal Navy for 6 weeks I began working at the call centre of a major bank in the financial world. I was a drunken, foul mouthed chef with anger issues and a split personality. This couldn't end well, could it?

Chapter 2

It would only be temporary. I told this to myself on a warm April morning as I walked into the call centre for the first time. I'd been told by a drunk down my new local pub that the centre was always looking for people and it was easy money and good bonuses. After six years of breaking my back on a warship, I looked forward to a job I could sit on my arse all day to do.

Each new group to the centre usually consisted of about 10-12 people. We were told on our first day that they didn't expect 50% of us to be there by the end of the week. They were right. We listened to examples of calls we would be taking the week after and it was car crash listening. Two people quit after hearing the calls and by the end of the week another four had been told they were not suited for the job. Have one week's wages and now fuck off. 40% of us were live on the phones with customers less than one week later. During my training I spent most of my time day dreaming about Karley our 23-year-old coach. She had big tits and a lovely bum that filled her pencil skirt perfectly to accompany a face that can only be described as 'cute as fuck'. Karley was the type of girl every heterosexual guy contemplates fucking within the first 10 seconds of meeting her. Hold on, scrub that, ANYONE who is sexually attracted to females would contemplate.

"So, sailor, it must have been hard for you all those years on that ship at sea with no female attention?"

Karley wasn't very discreet in her flirting and it was obvious, a little too obvious what her intentions were.

"Maybe no women but I had 307 guys to choose from to keep me warm every night."

The room burst into hysterics along with Karley who was doubled up in laughter and still teasing me with that perfect peach ass.

"You'll do alright here Ten, you'll fit right in."

Chapter 3

I was given the full birth name Tennyson Wilde. My mother wanted me to be called Jimmy after the famous Welsh boxer Jimmy Wilde, the ghost with the hammer in his hands. My father however being an ex-thug himself decided on Tennyson after reading *Idylls of the King*. After being named after such a renowned poet, I wasted my literary youth on porno magazines. I became somewhat of a master of obtaining porn as a youngster and then trading it for better magazines. I was a good little thief and found great ways of building my porn stash. I wasn't as good as Billy though. Billy was known in school as the Cock Mag King, a complete fucking perv with an extraordinary porn collection for a young teenage boy. Billy had some of the very finest printed pornography of the 1990s and was the envy of the school.

The name Tennyson was now only used when speaking to my Oldman, which these days could mean years. Everyone else shortened it to Ten, especially in Wales as every fucker has their name shortened. Richard becomes Rich, Philip becomes Phil, Thomas becomes Tom and Johnathan became Rubber Head after getting kicked out of a whore house for trying to put a condom over the prostitute's heads. The prozzy flipped out and Rubber Head got kicked the fuck out but he did get to take a lifelong nickname with him.

I took my final security tests on Friday to make sure I knew how to ID a phone customer correctly. It was easy enough as the calls we took were just the coaches in the other room pretending to be customers. They asked us easy stuff like balances and transactions, basic shit. The bank wanted us to pass as they needed bums on seats to sell their loans and credit cards for them. A few people couldn't handle the pressure of a soft, easy call with a coach and they were unequivocally told this wasn't a job for them. They would be paid for the rest of the week but don't bother coming back next week. It was brutal, it was dog eat dog and, in this place, I quickly found out that meant you could trust nobody. If you weren't making the bank money, they'd fucking eat you up and spit you out regardless of circumstances. After lunch on the Friday they read out a list of names and gave the following instructions.

"If your name is called, please follow the signs to the cafeteria where we can give you further instructions. Richard, Sadie, Jess, Mario and Tennyson. Thank you for the hard work this week please follow Karley."

As I got up to out with the others, I felt disappointed. Not because I didn't get the job but more for the fact, I didn't get the job 'any cunt could do' according to my new drinking buddy. Thanks for the pep talk my pisshead friend. I walked past Karley who could see my disappointment but still gave me a cheeky wink and smile. For fuck sakes I thought, I just been sacked after a week and you're still flirting.

"Don't look so disappointed sailor, follow me to the canteen."

Chapter 4

We were welcomed into the small cramped cafeteria that looked like a school dining hall just shitter and with more people who looked like they didn't want to be there. However, they did have 'comfy' chairs that they all seemed very proud of. A few mentioned with pride about the comfy canteen seats which was very fucking strange and more than a little bit creepy. We sat in the comfy chairs that we'd been directed to by a small feminine gentleman called Gerald, then we all awaited our fate. In a camp voice and full of stereotypically hand gestures Gerald announced, "You've all passed the week's training course, CONGRATULATIONS. So, let's all start smiling a little bit hey." I assumed Gerald was gay. He didn't come out and say he was gay but he just seemed, well, gay! A nice fella if a touch over excitable it turns out he was gay as he told me in front of a group of my workmates a few months later how he and his boyfriend had talked about me and my good looks. I think it may just have been the thought of my old sailor uniform that turned him on as my good looks had been drank and fought away years ago. I liked Gerald he was a good guy and he didn't take shit from anyone.

"Right guys and girls you will start Monday morning so not too drunk this weekend. Mario, Sadie and Richard you'll be going on the bereavement line, you will hear people call it the 'death line'. It's not as bad as it sounds. People will just call to report a death and then we can take action to get some of the debt paid off before that money becomes tied up." I was glad I didn't get that job.

"Jess and Tennyson, you two are selling you silver tongued assassins. Report to Leighton on sales downstairs Monday morning. Mario, Sadie and Richard come to the canteen."

Chapter 5

"Logged on at 7:55 please people, ready to take calls at 8," came Leighton's strong West Wales accent reverberating around my drunken and hungover swimming pool of a head.

"Apart from the two newbies, you two don't bother logging on just come to my desk at 8."

"Ok guys it's simple here. You have a points target to hit every month. If you sell well, you will meet your target. If you sell like fuck you will get a hell of a bonus each quarter as well." Leighton's words were more encouraging as I needed to earn some cash as I didn't have the Navy wiping my arse anymore. We'd been given certain things to look for when selling to customers, little signs. How much borrowing they already had, how much came into their account, how much went out and who it was going to, what direct debits they had set up, all these could be seen as tell-tale signs. Most importantly though was the behaviour score. If the BS was under 40 the customer would more than likely fail a credit scored application, waste an hour of someone's selling time and also end up giving us shit because their finances are shite. Like it's all our fault. DO NOT SELL to BS under 40!

Leighton continued trying to keep it undaunting and simple as possible, he came across as a decent guy from the way he conducted himself around Jess and myself.

"Rule of the team you two. When Jerome comes round, which he will a couple of times a day, just look busy. Pretend you're reading procedures off the screen or something. He normally leaves us alone after we pay him no attention the big-headed cunt. Our sales figures are the best in the centre so he doesn't really fuck with us."

There were 8 teams of 12 people, Leighton managed one of those teams, mine. Jerome managed the 8 team managers, therefore he managed all under the team managers as well.
He was a cocksucker. I had been warned.

Chapter 6

Jerome slithered over to the team all fake tan and fake muscles, lisping like a cunt. The turnover rate of staff was so high in the building that he couldn't be fucked meeting the new team members individually. He would just hold court for 5 minutes to confirm indeed, yes, he was a tremendous cocksucker, I was not lied to on that one. He'd do the usual shit of "say your name and something interesting about yourself" get to know each other bullshit. Jess went first. "My name's Jess, I'm 24 and have a child with my partner Nicola. An interesting fact about myself is that I got married to Nicola in a civil ceremony dressed as the groom. Nicola dressed as the groom as well and our friend Henry conducted the ceremony dressed as Alanis Morissette because he looks like her and we all love Alanis. It was a great day.''

Enter the cocksucker.

"Not very interesting is it, jumping on the bandwagon most of it. Married by a gay bloke, give me a break."
"Henry's not gay.''
"Yeah and he's not a minister either so it doesn't really count. Ok next on to the Army guy."

What a prick this guy was but I held my wise cracks as much as possible. "My name's Ten and I've just recently left the Royal Navy."

"No nicknames sailor boy, real names only."
"My name is Tennyson, shortened to Ten."
"What type of name is Tennyson? I've never heard of it."
"He was a poet Jerome."
"Well Mr Poet, tell us all something interesting about yourself we're all pretty busy here."

This fucking guy, I took the bait.

"I once downed a bottle of Jack Daniels in 8 seconds in Gibraltar and knocked a monkey out while going to the casino with the boys. I got witnesses who can verify that as well if you need and arrest records."
I did have witnesses to that but not punching the monkey, that was a lie. I did once see someone knock a fucker out up the rock though, for stealing his chips in 2003. With the hangover ripping my head to bits and my arsehole clenching for dear life as 30 pints of Guinness threaten to make a shitty appearance on my first proper day, I make an enemy of my new boss. He didn't like me and I certainly couldn't stand him.

"You talk funny Wilde, where you from?"
"Around."
"Another cocky ex-military big mouth hey?"
"I'm here to do a job not make friends Jerome."
"Well, I'll be taking a special interest in your stats Wilde."
"Appreciate that son, thanks for looking out for me."
"I'm your boss not one of your drinking pals, don't call me son."
"Well, I'm your employee and I may have to pay a visit to my union rep if this carries on."
"Gonna go crying to the union? I thought you military lot were supposed to be hardcases, fucking whinge bags more like."
"I never said I was a hardcase Jerome but please feel free to do your due diligence on me and we can take it from there."

Jerome walked off with a grin on his face and called me a twat under his breath but loud enough that everyone heard. He did however do a little bit of due diligence on me later, through social media and talking to his steroid freak friends. It's a small city and as it turns out I'd battered two of his mates when I was a teenager in a nightclub called Quids Inn. I don't remember too many of my drunken brawls but I specifically remembered this one as it happened in the packed nightclub toilets. Two guys attacked me while I was taking a piss and instinct kicked in. I was manic and never fought better, probably because my cock was still hanging out when I was attacked from behind. These two toilet lurking wank stains (Jerome's friends) had seen me as an easy target as I was only weighing about 147lbs but I was training hard at the time and on the cusp of signing papers to turn professional. I connected with about 20 punches in less than 10 seconds to both these fuckers faces, all while my dick was still hanging out of my pants. My power and hand speed were more than decent for a skinny little white kid. I never signed the professional papers, I got caught up in the street reputation bullshit and in a small city it always ends up catching up with you.

Leighton pulled me to one side.
"He's an arsehole Ten don't worry about him. Just hit your targets and make your sales and he'll stay off your back."
 "Will do Leighton, thanks."
"And cut it with the Leighton shit, call me Late."

Jerome never talked big to me again but he did wind me up almost everyday by just being an egotistical cunt who took pleasure in bullying vulnerable people. I was nowhere near the fighter I used to be but I would have still fucked Jerome up within 10-15 seconds, and he knew it, and he knew I knew it as well.

Chapter 7

The calls came in thick and fast. There was no time to think there was only time to react, like they had programmed us to do.
Get the customer's profile screen up, check the behavior score. Over 40??? 67, YES guaranteed sale if I can hook the customer. What haven't you got Mr Customer, what can I con you into signing up for? What haven't you got that you don't need that I can make you take out? Credit Card, good bonus points there and an easy sale too. 0% interest for 12 months and then 14.9% APR variable after that with the option of a free balance transfer. It was a good deal and good points in the bag for me. Next call. Get the customer profile screen up, check the BS, over 40??? 33!!!! Get the fuck off my phone you time waster. What do you want? Your balance? It's £26.19 in credit. Anything else? No? Good, now fuck off so I can sell to a decent account.

Next call, same as always check the BS. 48. Not a great BS for selling so it's instead time to play on the customer's fears and put things into their head. Just remember you as a customer don't know we've got a BS on you and we'll never tell you what it is either. We make the rules not you. 48 BS???? I hold all the Ace's motherfucker; you need to consolidate your credit card and overdraft into a loan. Why? Well because at 11.9% APR you won't get a better deal elsewhere shitbag. And by the way Mr Shitbag if your BS was 51 that rate would have been 8.9% but I'm not gonna tell you that sucker. YOU DON'T WANT THE LOAN??? That's ok Mr Shitbag let me tell you why you will take the loan out. At the end of this call your overdraft interest rate will increase from 3.1% to 5.1% and your credit card will no longer qualify for the bonus 5.5% rate you've been enjoying for 2 years. Unfortunately, Mr Shitbag your credit card rate will now go up to 14% and overall your monthly payments will increase by approximately £109.73. If you get off the phone today without the loan I have generously offered you. What's that Mr Shitbag? You now want the loan? Thank you, I'll just put you through to the loans department so they can fuck with your head some more and tie you up to a good loan for the bank. Thank you Mr Shitbag, yes goodbye to you as well sucker. Next call.

This would be how my day would go, repetitive shit for about two hours then a cigarette break. We had a 15 minute cigarette break twice a day, one in the morning before lunch and one after lunch. As we worked shifts, sometimes we wouldn't start until 2pm and finish at 10pm so the cigarette breaks became an afternoon/night split. The smoking shelter was an old disused bus stop that was rusty and leaking. The plastic see through screens covered in dirt, dust and the constant nicotine cloud that squatted there. You could see out but you couldn't see in. During my 15 minutes I would suck down two pre rolled cigs using the burning ambers of the first to light the second cig to give me the hit I required to complete another two hours on the phone. The smoking shelter conversations deviated from politics, to customers, to managers being dicks, to weekend drinking and shagging exploits. But in the smoking shelter you had to always be aware of your surroundings, this is where the backstabbers lurk. Hanging on people's words like a fly sniffing round some shit. Sometimes these motherfuckers didn't even smoke, they just came as they knew that's where you learned the good information. The good shit.

Then back on the phones for another two hours. Another round of behavior score bingo with the telephone Nazis but we didn't care what colour your skin was, half our centre was Asian. We just cared about the colour of your money and how much we could take off you while also looking at the same time about how much debt we could tie you up to for the next 5-10 years.

Then we went to lunch.

Chapter 8

Lunch

A one-hour lunchbreak was far too long in this place, I would have been good with 20 minutes, so I could have fucked off home 40 minutes early to get on the beer. Approximately 45 minutes of that lunch break was spent in the smoking shelter, or on a nice day, within the designated smoking area around the shelter. I'd buy an overpriced meal deal from the canteen and take it back to my desk just as my lunch break was about to end. I'd put my headset back on and slowly eat my lunch before I started taking calls again as I wasn't prepared to let eating interfere with my smoking lunch break. After 45 minutes straight in the smoking shelter you were either buzzing or suicidal before you went back in to finish your shift. Sit down, go ready, take calls. Another afternoon of behaviour score bingo.

Chapter 9

I'd swapped an 8-digit military ID card for an 8-digit bank ID. Another soulless photograph I had to look at everyday and a number that would be stamped in my psyche forever. I wasn't very superstitious but my bank ID card would be facedown on my desk all day, everyday, for every year I was there. I couldn't look at my photo while talking to customers. Maybe I was ashamed of what my job involved; I don't know but every morning I would flip my ID so I didn't have to look at myself doing a job I hated.

I was now a storm trooper for the financial evil empire. We roamed the telephone lines like a bunch of bullies. We were the conquerors of integrity and selling was king. If they didn't want it? Fuck um. Force them into it. Bully them, scare them, threaten them, just get that fucking sale. Then get another. And another. Get another and win a bottle of wine. The procedures and scripts we had to follow and read out to customers were dogshit and didn't make sense to us half the time let alone the customers. Procedures took 3 years to be implemented due to a factory full of corporate red tape bullshit. By the time the procedures went live they were already outdated and not fit for purpose. It was a circus run by the people with the most money and the most shit between their ears.

"Late, this customer wants his charges back."
"Have you checked your procedures Ten?"
"Yes mate, he doesn't qualify for a refund as there's no bank error but he's kicking off here."
"I don't give a fuck if he's kicking off or not, if he doesn't qualify for a refund, he's not getting one. Sell him a loan."

Sell him a loan? Sell him a fucking loan? The guys about to kill someone or have a heart attack while cursing me out and you want me to sell him a loan. The unjustified charges we as a bank put on him are what's caused this argument. We have somehow justified the charges and then made the customer out to be the bad guy. And now I'm supposed to sell the fucker a loan? 7 times out of 10 I could lie to a customer and get them to believe it was actually their fault. Not this guy though, he was having none of it. Time for silver tongue Tennyson to take care of this fuck nugget. Bullshit baffles brains so I just basically talked shit to the customer until they fuck off or buy a product off me. But let me put you on hold first so I can look over your account.

"Thank you for waiting Mr Fuck Nugget, sorry for keeping you waiting. Ok I've looked through your account and I've also spoken to our credit control department. They are concerned about your account and the lack of incoming funds to reduce your overdrawn balance."

I was lying, I didn't go and speak to anyone I just sat there for 2 minutes while customer was on hold listening to shit hold music.

"I'm not going to refund your charges today Mr Fuck Nugget but I am going to give you access to an overdraft facility for free. This will cover the charges going out that we will still take, and we will allow you to max your overdraft out and then we'll fuck you over again. I know this will fuck up your life for the next couple of years but at least I won a bottle of wine for putting an overdraft on your account that you didn't even ask for."

This was mis-selling at its finest and I was a Master as I ended the call, "My pleasure Mr Fuck Nugget, you too. Merry Christmas to you as well, and have a fuck nugget new year with your fuck nugget wife and your fuck nugget kids. Goodbye Mr Fuck Nugget, thanks for the sale and wine."

Chapter 10

I came in to the office hung over most mornings. As the people were used to seeing me like this nobody really looked twice. I showered and shaved each morning, as much to try and sober myself up as it was to clean myself. It worked in the Navy and my drinking had transferred seamlessly from military to civvy street. I had become an Olympic standard drinker. Usain Bolt may do me over 100 metres but would he be able to drink 20 pints of lager then have a race? No chance. I'd done some of my best running while escaping from cops, thugs or bouncers I'd pissed off at 2am completely shitfaced. My boxing career ended in the Navy partly due to my drinking and partly due to being a chef and those motherfuckers working us to death with very little downtime or adequate facilities for training. I was disappointed by the drinking capabilities of the call centre crew, most were lightweights who were pissed after 2 hours. Cocaine wasn't really needed in the Navy as we were hardcore drinkers but I found the civvies needed to bang more of that shit up their noses to carry on drinking. I didn't need drugs but I liked them. Due to random drug tests in the military, I largely abstained, however over the years I did fuck up a few times with weed, cocaine and heroin. I'd sniffed lines of cocaine off the arses of pretty whores in a Times Square bar that doubled as a whore house. My shipmate, Scottish Al, found the place the dirty cunt. NYC was a great run ashore. RIP Scottish Al.

I'd smoked heroin on the midnight train from Portsmouth to Swansea while shitfaced on white cider and taken under the wing of a black Cardiff drug dealer called Percy for the 55 minutes train ride from Cardiff to Swansea. Percy had a large scar running down the side of his face caused by a samurai sword attack from a rival drug gang a few years before. I had no reason to not believe Percy's stories, he certainly looked the real deal standing well over 6 foot and a muscular build for a smackhead.

"Come out with me tonight Ten, we'll sell all this shit and save some for ourselves, go partying then and get some pussy."
I made my excuses as I didn't fancy strutting around my home city pumping smack with a Cardiff geezer who was obviously going to be kicking some poor fucker's head in later.

"For a Jack bastard you're alright Ten. Got a few Jack fuckers down here that owe me some cash. I won't be as friendly to them tonight."
We shook hands, exchanged numbers and after leaving the train station we went our separate ways, thank fuck. While in the toilets of a shitty

commuter train racing through the South Wales valleys, I chased the dragon for the final time. I never saw Percy again.

Chapter 11

Even though I was earning decent money in work, I didn't waste it on such things as clothes or women. My money was for drinking and I could drink wearing a fucking bin bag if I wanted. I didn't struggle for female attention but I wasn't looking for any sort of relationship that would jeopardise the partying I was enjoying at the moment with no fear of a random drugs test to fuck me over.

I had a car but only used it when I really needed it, or if it was an emergency like running out of booze late at night. I hadn't been capable of passing a breathalyzer for over 6 years. Even if I had two days break (which was unheard of) I was still registering a score on the breathalyzer. I lived close enough to work, the shops and the gym. I was able to walk everywhere I needed. You can't get an 18 month ban for doing a speed wobble walking down the street. Yes, I did drink drive on numerous occasions, mostly when I'd run out of alcohol late at night. I wasn't proud of this fact but like fuck was I walking down there. The crazy mind of an alcoholic. I wouldn't drive when I was soberish due to the fear of being pulled by the cops but as soon as the booze ran out, FUCK THE LICENCE!

As a functioning alcoholic a routine is critical. However, as a functioning alcoholic the routine is often the thing that became the victim of the chaos that engulfed it. I mean it's hard to get up for a 6:30am alarm for work when you're in the police cells sleeping on a blue crashmat and an itchy, piss smelling blanket is keeping you warm. The moment I open my eyes and the familiar surroundings become apparent I quickly realized two things.

1) I won't be going to work today.

2) I can't go anywhere until the copper comes to get me.
Through forced imprisonment I know I can't go anywhere or do anything. I feel freedom and pull the piss-stained itchy blanket back up to my chin and go back to sleep.

Chapter 12

Glug strutted back to his desk 7 minutes late off his 15-minute break for the second time of the day. Laughing and joking Glug didn't give a fuck but I could see Leighton was boiling up inside. He had a habit or maybe some form of Tourette's that would cause him to blurt out what he was thinking when it was pretty obvious he should have been keeping those thoughts to himself.

"Cancer lunged cunt."

Glug didn't break stride as he burst into fits of hysterical laughter after being insulted by Leighton.

"Glug, you're fucking late back from break again. What the fuck? Do you try and push my buttons?"
"Hahahaha sorry Late." Glug is visibly stoned as fuck when he returns to his desk, still giggling at being called a cancer lunged cunt.

"Ten. Ten, swap places with Glug for me, he's a pain in the ass."
"No chance Late. I've got a spot here where the sun doesn't shine on my screen, I'm not moving."

I didn't mind moving but on this occasion I was sat opposite Karley and our flirting had continued after she trained me up and then she joined our team. I felt I was close to getting her clothes off and laying a naked bare ass back hander across that peachy ass she paraded in front of my

23

eyes. I wonder if it moves like she makes it move when she comes and sits on my desk.

"Sorry Late," Glug's finally stopped laughing.
"There was some top banter going on in the smoking shelter, funny as fuck," he's laughing again and Leighton's losing his shit.
"I don't give a fuck about the conversation quality. 15 minutes your break is! Stop taking the piss."

Glug slouches back into his chair still with a massive grin on his face and obviously mischief in mind. Leighton had already said the final word but decided he wanted to put the cherry on top.

"You need to stop smoking Glug. Dim Ysmygu."

Dim Ysmygu (dim Us-Muggy) is a Welsh command, no smoking! Without missing a beat Glug shot back.

"Rydw i'n hoffi ysmygu." (rud oow in hoffi us-muggy). I like smoking.

"Dim ysmygu."
"Rydw i'n hoffi ysmygu."
"Dim ysmygu."
"Rydw i'n hoffi ysmygu."

Leighton wasn't even looking at Glug now as he knew as soon as eye contact was made it was over. Glug would roast him. Leighton didn't take his eyes from his screen.

"Dim ysmygu."
"Rydw i'n hoffi ysmygu."
"Dim ysmygu."
"Rydw i'n hoffi ysmygu."

"Dim ysmygu."
"Rydw i'n hoffi ysmygu."
"Dim fucking ysmygu."
"For fuck sakes Late, rydw i'n hoffi fucking ysmygu."
"Dim fucking ysmygu."
"Rydw i'n hoffi fucking ysmygu."

On and on like a pair of 30-year-old kids, back and forth until Leighton finally caved in.

"Right get back on the phone Glug you're pissing me off now and the queues are fucking red status. Take some fucking calls before Jerome comes over and starts moaning. You have to do your one to one as well."

"Time off the phone that is Late, get to spend an hour with you" an excited Glug slurred out in his stoner tones.

"Yeah don't remind me. I've got to psyche myself up to spend an hour with you talking shit." Again, Leighton's eyes didn't move from his screen as he talked. I sat next to Glug. Karley sat opposite me and Sadie sat next to her, so there was always some sort of inappropriate banter being thrown around. 60% of this came directly from Karley, she had a filthy mouth. Glug changed the code on his computer from 662 which was the break code to Go Ready, which meant calls would come through.

"Good afternoon Mr Floyd, you're through to Richard. How can I help you today?" Glug had the telephone voice, the vibe and an easy going way about him that had the customers eating shit out of his hand. When we would listen in to each other, we would only hear what we as employees were saying, we couldn't hear the customer so we'd just assume what that had said from the responses given. Glug was in full flow. "Yes sir, oh indeed Mr Floyd. Yes sir, I'm more of a Salvidor Dali fan myself, yes Mr Floyd.'' Glug was good. "South Wales Mr Floyd. Yes, it is a beautiful part of the world. Yes, uh huh, yes. A little bit Mr Floyd. Rydw i'n hoffi ysmygu. No I'm not fluent Mr Floyd but enough to get a C in my GCSEs.''

Leighton sat at his desk with his head in his hands. Again talking out loud when it probably should have been his inside voice. "For fuck sakes Lord. What did I do to deserve this cunt?''

Call comes through.

"Good afternoon Mrs Patel, you're speaking to Richard, how can I help you today? Thank you Mrs Patel I'm actually having a wonderful day, thank you for asking. Yes I am Welsh, I speak a little. Would you like to hear some?''

I don't think I need to carry on in order to tell how the rest of that call went. It was entertaining for everyone apart from Late. Stuff like this happened day in, day out, whenever Glug was working. He had us in tears of utter disbelief and also fits of hysterics at least twice a day. Jerome let Glug do what he wanted as he smashed all his sales targets and in doing so became one of Jerome's golden geese for a highly respectable bonus each quarter.

"Did he really just say that?'' was a phrase most used by visitors to our team. Glug was a good guy and as I've said he didn't give a fuck.

I left Glug and Late to their Laurel & Hardy routine while I put in a little more groundwork with Karley and getting into her knickers. It wouldn't be long.

Chapter 13

Pacman nudged me with his elbow. "Hey Ten, check him out. He's got a head like a shark," nodding towards a guy about 20 yards away. "He certainly does pal. Guess what his nickname is? Sharkhead!" Pacman burst into fits of laughter while blurting out "FUCK OFF," forgetting we could be overheard by at least 12 live calls to customers. The reaction I got from Pacman brightened my day and I laughed hard as well, mostly due to his reaction. As he was a new boy on the floor I decided he should probably meet the Shark as I had a good feeling about Pacman compared to the usual bunch of dicks we got lumbered with.

"SHARKHEAD. Sharkey boy, come here son, come over here and meet Pacman." As the shark approached Pacman turned and asked me "so why you lot call me Pacman Ten?" Without hesitation as I knew he was a cool kid and not a grass I told him straight. "We call you Pacman cos you got a big mouth bud. Got a mouth like the fucking Joker. Lucky we didn't call you Sharkmouth." Shark got close and opened his mouth for the Swansea accent and lingo to come spilling out.

"Alright Ten, what's happening son? How's tricks? Shagging or what? Pissed last night son?" This was a usual type of greeting from Sharkhead. Machine gun speed questions flying out of his mouth about anything dirty or dodgy.

"I'm all good Sharkey boy, well as good as I can be in this fucking place, you knows the score son. This is Pacman one of the new boys, he's alright shark. He plays football with Stevie T and Skips, they both told me he's a good guy, trustworthy and not a snitch."

Sharkhead slowly turned that fucking bizarre human sharkhead and looked Pacman dead in the eyes. "Pacman??? I would have called you letterbox mouth! Fucking hell son, that's a 3 cock mouth you got there. Get down the docks, earn yourself a few quid.'' The freestyle rhetoric of abuse hit Pacman square in the face and he was laughing so hard he almost was crying, which in turn set Sharkhead off too.

The shark was a natural comedian and when he got on a roll he could reduce crowds of 30 or 40 people into a bunch of giggling wrecks. A talented guy and hell of a character. When the two new besties had stopped laughing and fucking about Shark went into some details of his morning on the phone.

"Skitzo is contagious today fellas. Fucking managers, fucking customers, fucking girlfriend texting. They all doing my fucking head in. I wish they all had one neck so I could wrap my hands around it and choke them all out, in one go.''

"You hitting your targets though Shark?'' I enquired as I knew he was a good bonus earner. If I was anywhere near Shark's stats I knew I'd get a decent bonus.

"Smashed the targets Ten, in the first two weeks of the quarter, dodgy re-gens.''

Re-gens or regeneration of savings was where the bonus points lay. There was gold there and we tried to mine it all. If a customer hadn't put money in their savings account for a while our job was to gently persuade them to do so. We would get them to move money from their current accounts into their savings, BUT. We would only get the points if they kept the funds in the savings for over 30 days. We would just tell the customers bullshit about added interest and all that shite but in reality we told the fuckers anything just so we got our re-gen points. There were a few dodgy fuckers amongst us that would keep a record of customer details in order to check every month. We knew they had auto sweeps into the savings accounts so we updated those as well. Didn't even move the money or speak to the customer, we'd just check the account and bag the points. Some of the guys and girls in the place had fucking books full of customer details they would check on a daily basis. The managers, and their managers and the big managers at the top knew what we were up to, it was a running joke for fuck sakes. At least twice a week Jerome would come over and make a joke about our dodgy re-gens and how our team always hit target in the first 10 days of each quarter. Every quarter. Every team member. Without fail.

From 2007 to 2010 I averaged a quarterly bonus of about £2500 which was up there with the top performers in the centre. An older lady who'd seen my selling potential taught me a few tricks of the re-gen trade, some of the dark arts. Each quarter she would have a bonus over double to mine.

We had to be careful though as there were plenty of jobsworths and grasses in the building who thrived on dropping people in the shit. Once each individual on the team hit target we then eased off on the dodgy shit to avoid suspicion. Sharkhead hated the grasses, "I hear you Ten, it's the right way to do it son. Plus, they're dead points anyway as you're just topping up an already full jar of points. Pacman was listening intently to our conversation and learning the unwritten rules of getting away with shit before the conversation turned to other things.

"Ten, you going to the Xmas party? Go as Bad Santa. That role was made for you, you pisshead cunt."
"Hahaha yeah nice one Shark. Prick. Yeah I'm going bud but not doing fancy dress, fuck that. You dressing up Shark? Go as a dolphin."
"Go as Sloth from The Goonies ya sharkhead fuck!!!"

Pacman's confidence, bolstered by being vouched for by me took him to new heights as he roasted the shark in a manner that Sharkhead loved. "Make sure this cunt comes Ten, we'll have a good laugh and get drunk as fuck." Sharkhead's fun could be dangerous. He didn't drink on the weekdays but would get fucked up every weekend. Last year's Xmas party was no different to Shark. In his own words "coming out of a drunken 3-hour blackout hanging out the back of a tattooed arse. It felt soft, round and smooth so I tried to keep the rhythm I'd found myself in. Like a drunken pornographic conga line." Shark had once told Karley, Jess and myself about his fantasy of Deirdre Barlow. He talked excitedly about "the scraggy neck temptress with bottle top glasses. Always in The Rovers getting drunk. Get her to fuck Ken Barlow off then a stroll down Coronation Street for drunken sex with the chicken necked Northern minx." I'd heard this charade from Shark before but it was still funny. Jess and Karley lapped it up, laughing like a couple of school kids.

The girls on our team were a measuring stick of what we could get away with saying. It was pointless really as they were worse than us and had language as bad as anything I experience in the Navy. Karley had a dirty mind. Her mind was so dirty it made the feet of a shithouse rat look clean. I had to get into bed with her, I had no doubts she felt the same as she often told me so, half joking half serious.

We'd been chatting to Sharkhead for a while and it was time for us all to get on with our day now. "Come on then Pacman let's get you back on the phone pal. That prick Jerome walking round now and I can't be fucked speaking to the cunt about Manchester fucking United."
The Shark wasn't a fan of Jerome either as one of his cousins was married to him, Starr. Jerome treated Starr like shit and a couple of years ago she'd come in with a blackeye. Sharkhead followed him into the back carpark after one shift and tuned him up pretty good. No witnesses. That's all the Shark ever said about the incident, no witnesses. Nothing else, ever, apart from, no witnesses.
Jerome never hit his wife again, well she never came into work battered again I suppose that doesn't guarantee he didn't hit her again. Anyway

Jerome was well aware of Sharkhead and his family so he knew any physicality would be paid back with interest. Even though the beatings stopped the cheating got worse and eventually Jerome would take pleasure in belittling Starr in front of everyone.

"I still don't give that prick the time of day Ten, hate the guy."

"Time of day? I wouldn't give him the stink off my shit the fucking ball bag. Saggy titted, roid head fuck. I'm quite jealous you got to give him a few slaps Shark."

With a wink and a nod of the head Sharkhead looks at me before walking off. "No witnesses Ten, no witnesses."

Chapter 14

Conversations with death, within dreams, within reality. Holding on to hope but losing grip of my sanity. Complexities of the mind with the distraction of emotions, lightening shadow dreams I have but the ether taste don't fade away. I'm hearing sounds in colour. Colours that I didn't even know existed. I can taste when the voices are about to make an appearance.

The Angel, The Devil, The Referee and me. The four voices of the Apocalypse.

The voices in my head used my mouth as a way to communicate their thoughts and opinions, mostly about drink. This would end up in an argument most of the time and even though it was my body and mind I still usually ended up losing. I was normally pretty discreet with my talking to voices and shit like that but if you did see me walking by the river or most of the time down the drink aisle in the supermarket, it would look like I was arguing with myself. I wasn't. I was actually part of a 4-way conversation with four completely different personalities involved. Each voice thought they knew what was best for me. So 'Me' quickly became 'Us' and we took it from there. These guys were in my head, they had ringside seats for the demise of my mind through drink.

Now don't get me wrong. I wasn't constantly talking to voices or acting mad. 95% of the time I spoke to the voices it was about alcohol but unfortunately, I was drinking on a daily basis so the conversations became more frequent and intense. I didn't even think of them as voices anymore but rather an extension of my psyche. I didn't have to drink for them to talk to me, most of the time I was actually sober and we would then talk about getting me drunk. It would always start about drink but then morph into everything on the table. Life, death, love, hate. The voices of the apocalypse were experts on all.
Did I class them as guardian angels? Maybe. I think it was more a case of different parts of my brain fighting an endless war for custody of my soul. I drank everyday so we talked everyday. A Rorschach jigsaw puzzle of a mind which made me sometimes think, which voice did I really belong to, if any of them, even mine. Twisting conversations flow, sometimes with a piano soundtrack just to nail the utter madness of the situation. Some of these conversations ended up saving my life but most just ended up with me getting drunk or drunker than I already was. The devil didn't always win but in terms of stats he was putting up some Michael Jordan numbers, an incredible win ratio that saw me shitfaced more often than not.

It was a Sunday night and I was pissed. I'd been drunk as fuck all weekend. I had to work at 8am so that meant getting up at 6:30am to walk the hangover off when I leave my house at 7:24am.
I'd arrive at my desk at 7:46am and blag my way through another shift and another £80 in my pocket. And then the voices started again.

"SO SUNDAY NIGHT AND YOUR FUCKING HAMMERED AGAIN FOR FUCK SAKES TEN DO YOU REMEMBER LAST MONDAY? IT WAS A FUCKING NIGHTMARE REMEMBER?"

Now you would have thought it would have been the angel who jumped in first to spoil the fun but it wasn't, it was the Ref. Angel, or Gel as I called him was cool and didn't stick his nose in unless asked. He would when he was concerned about my health but most of the time he knew it was a losing battle. He let a lot of shit slide and kept his mouth shut. Ref however was foul mothed and argumentative. He loved to pick a fight and was often guilty of causing an argument when it wasn't needed, like here.

"Yeah I remember last Monday but it's too late now anyway as we're already fucked up," I knew I was fucked up as soon as I started referring to myself as us rather than I.
Gel would come in and try to reason, **"Ten that's not right man, you can just knock it on the head for tonight and tomorrow won't be as bad."** Then every fucker gets involved.

(Me) Tomorrow's fucked already
(Dev) *Certainly is bud, get those cans down you. How many we got left?*
(Me) We got 5 big cans left. It's 19:55 so these will last until about 21:45, after that we're fucked
(Dev) *Fucking heads or tails for a trip down the off licence then*
(Ref) NO FUCKING CHANCE WE AINT GOING THROUGH THIS SHIT AGAIN TONIGHT WE'VE HAD IT ALL WEEKEND
(Me) Look we'll drink these cans and see what time we finish and then take it from there. Now fuck off and let me watch a movie

21:15

(Dev) *Last can boys and it's still early. Trip to the off licence or what?*

33

(Me) Sounds good to me, let's go

(Ref) SOUNDS GOOD? YOU CAN HARDLY SPEAK LET ALONE HEAR YOU FUCKING IMBECILE

(Me) Fuck you!

(Dev) *Fuck who?*

(Me) Fuck him!

(Ref) FUCK ME?

(Me) Fuck you!

(Ref) FUCK YOU!!!

(Dev) *More drink!*

(Me) Yes!!!

(Ref) FUCK YOU BOTH!!!

(Gel) **Look guys we'll get 4 cans down the shop so we can stop arguing.**

(Dev) *8*

(Ref) SEE!!! FUCKING PUSHING NEVER HAPPY WITH A COMPROMISE ALWAYS TRYING TO CUNT SOMEONE OFF

(Dev) *I'll compromise at 8. If I wanted to be a cunt I'd push it to 10 as I'm owed 2 cans from the last time I backed down''*

(Ref) THAT'S A FUCKING LIE! FIRSTLY YOU NEVER BACK DOWN YOU JUST GET OUTNUMBERED 4 CANS TONIGHT IS FAIR

(Dev) *8*

(Ref) 4 AND I'M NOT BUDGING ON THAT

(Me) Heads or tails for it then?

(Dev) *Do it! Tails for Wales never fails.*

If we're playing heads or tails it means I'll be going and getting more cans than is advisable. The coin toss charade will continue to be played until 'tails for Wales' lands. If we're losing Dev will push for best of 3, best of 5, best of 7. On and on until we win. Am I mentally ill?

(Ref) YES YOU ARE FUCKING MENTALLY ILL WHY THE FUCK PLAY THE GAME? YOU KNOW YOU'LL BE GOING REGARDLESS OF THE OUTCOME

OF THE COIN TOSS FARCE FUCK THE COIN TOSS CIRCUS JUST GO YOU KNOW YOU EVENTUALLY WILL ANYWAY

No...The game has to be played. We needed the win to justify our decision even though the result would be completely fixed for me and Dev to win.

This was how the majority of the conversations went. Nights ended and mornings began but there was never a winner, just a lot of bad feelings and "I told you so's. **I told you so's.** *I told you so's* and I TOLD YOU SO'S.'' The only winner was alcohol. It was always the only winner, he won everytime. The 4 voices of the apocalypse would still be drawn back to the alcohol as if it was the giver of life. We'd convene again later and chat. We'd win again later, and lose again. We already knew this. We'd play another rigged game of heads or tails and use the outcome of a fixed game to hopefully glue together the pieces of a broken mind.

6:30am. Alarm goes off.

I hope I didn't play heads or tails last night.

Chapter 15

Monday mornings in work meant one thing, Power Hours. As the bank didn't complete lending applications on the weekend we had a massive push for sales on the next working day to make up for the wasted sales of the weekend. A Power Hour was basically a centre wide competition to see who could sell the most of the banks shit product to sucker customers within a 1 hour time frame. Due to the bank's greed they were called Power Hours but they normally went for 2 hours.

There were prizes to be won that consisted of two things, alcohol or finishing work early. As you've probably guessed I liked my free booze and going home to rattle about in an empty house sober didn't really appeal to me. Although, if alcohol wasn't on offer or there was a shit selection for my alcoholic palate to enjoy, I would take the time off and head to the pub. Loads of people were deadly serious about winning these Power Hours. Many brought in left over coke from the weekend to bang up their noses down in the toilets to give them that edge when selling. You call a major worldwide financial institution only to be greeted by a motor mouthed cocaine freak trying to sell you any piece of shit lending product while at the same time completely side stepping the customers original reason for calling. You couldn't make this shit up, it was madness!!! I personally never used cocaine in work. I was already a social hand grenade and to be honest with you I didn't need it. I was a fucking good sales person naturally. That's not being arrogant or big headed it was just facts. Check the stats, check my numbers, check my compensation history, ask my fucking customers.

I didn't fuck about and would regularly outsell my whole team put together, even with a stinking hangover.

Pacman headed to the toilets with Sadie, our team's wild child. Sadie was like me as in she hated her job but was really fucking good at it. She went for her usual pre Power Hour line of charlie and took Pacman with her. I don't know if they had already or not BUT these two had to fuck. The sexual chemistry between two young people was sometimes actually awkward to be around and I'd told Sadie a few times just to take him home and fuck his brains out. They both returned from the toilets laughing and chatting shit, high on terrible cocaine that was underpriced so it was obvious it was shite.

10:55 and Leighton gave us the usual Power Hour buzz meeting and motivational speech.

"Right you lot, you know the score. Sell, sell and fucking sell. I got loads of booze and time off to give away and it be nice to have some winners off this team this week that aren't Sadie or Ten."

"Ten's a fucking cheat Late, he updates stuff he hasn't even mentioned to customers."

"Fuck you Glug that's bullshit man. You've heard me sell. I sell the fuckers a loan and just as I put them through to complete the loan I say that the rep they will speak to MAY discuss other products like overdrafts, credit cards, mortgages, insurance, account upgrades, foreign currency, pensions. As long as I mention then I can update them so fuck you!"

Glug was still not impressed by my shady selling tactics having a blind eye turned to them and wouldn't let it go. I was laughing by now as I could see Glug getting wound up.

"Look at him Late, fucking laughing too, the dodgy Del Boy motherfucker!"

"I'm a silver tongued devil Glug, just ask your mother."

"Fuck you Ten!!!"

The banter continued until 10:59 when Leighton announced "almost 11 people. Let's sell some shit and keep that fucking bell end Jerome off our backs." When everyone takes their first call it's like being a kid in a sweet shop as we're all rushing to sell any bit of shit just to get on the board. Sadie was flying already and racked up three sales off her first call. I needed to sort my shit out and catch up quick. I looked over to Pacman who was red and sweating like fuck. Not used to taking coke and especially not in work he started having a panic attack.

"Hey Pacman, you good? You look fucked mate, drink some water, keep your head down."

My medical advice didn't work as Pacman turned his worried face to me and started to quietly freak out.
"Fucking hell Ten, I've done it now. Coked up in work, they'll fucking sack me. I'm fucked Ten, I'm fucked."
"You're not fucked mate, about 20% of the floor is on some sort of chemical stimulant for this Power Hour. Just keep your head down, you'll be good in 20 minutes bud." I couldn't think of anything else to say but it didn't calm Pacman as his panic continued.

"Jesus Christ oh Jesus what the fuck."

Leighton could hear Pacman talking but couldn't make out what he was on about. "Pacman, you ok? What's up? Who are you talking to?" Pacman didn't hear Late he just carried on with his Jesus Christs.

"Jesus? You've got fucking Jesus on the phone? Ask him if he wants a credit card."

Leighton's easy-going manner and jokes calmed the situation as we all had a bit of a cathartic laugh to ease the tension. Pacman regained his composure and completed the Power Hour managing to sell absolutely fuck all. Sadie won the time off as per usual and was actually already packing her stuff to go home halfway through the competition.
Glug won the booze and took great pleasure in winding me up about it for the rest of the afternoon.

"Fuck you Del Boy, couldn't cheat your way to the booze this week hey?" Glug and me were good pals and loved the banter.
"I had to let you win some time Glug, don't wanna be accused of bullying you, you fucking stoner."

Glug may have won the booze, Sadie may have won the time off but I got to speak to Mrs Thedig. And if I got given the choice again, I wouldn't change it. Well, I would have changed my seat so I didn't have to look after our baby Scarface having a coke melt down. Life is about opportunities and keeping your eyes and ears open for these times. Some people are too busy trying to talk through their own perception of self-importance to actually listen to a different point of view, a different story, a new opportunity. Not me. I was open to any dodgy or dirty scam I could get involved with. If it was going to involve my pockets getting fatter with cash, sign me up. And so it went.

"Good morning Mrs Thedig, my names Tennyson. How can I help you today?"

Chapter 16

Everyone had been excited about the boxing match due to take place in a few weeks. Boxing fans, casual boxing fans, football fans, rugby fans, well every fucker really. Everyone had an opinion on the outcome and most people were siding with the former champ to win by knock out. Now unfortunately the names of the fighters will remain anonymous and the reason will become apparent when we proceed. The former champ was making a comeback after two years out of the ring. When I say former champ I don't mean some alphabet belt champ, I'm talking about THE champ, the top dog! The only thing that concerned me was how much drinking and shagging and partying had he done in the two years since retirement? Hold on, hold on. Let me take you back to explain this properly.

Six weeks before the fight I took a call from a customer.
"Good morning Mrs Thedig, blah blah blah."

Anyway, it turns out Mrs Thedig was the personal assistant to the champ and a sort of mother figure too. She had called up to pay one of the champs ridiculously big credit card bills. Mrs Thedig was a nice lady who was easy to talk to so the conversation flowed freely. My genuine interest in the champ's career made the proud mum in Mrs Thedig to make an appearance as she talked about all his achievements. As she was so comfortable she started telling me things about the champ she probably shouldn't have, but I gobbled it all up like a student thirsting for more knowledge. Mrs Thedig was concerned. She said the champ hadn't been training and was out of shape with six weeks to go. By the looks of his credit card bill he'd been trying to drink, fuck and gamble anything he could get his hands on. I was told about certain twitches and reactions the champ would give off when nervous or in trouble. She didn't like the weight drain either as it made him look gaunt and ill. Boxing fans had seen the champ struggle with weight in the past and all his losses or bad performances were down to being out of shape. The conversation had sparked the gambler in me.

"Have a great day Mrs Thedig, please give the champ my best wishes for the fight, I hope he can win."

I stayed in code and didn't take another call until I'd had a good snoop around this fucker's account looking for signs. It turns out he loved a gamble, fucking LOVED it! Plenty of wins but also loads of losses, big ones too.

"He's back for the cash!"

"What's that Ten?"

"Oh nothing, sorry Late, just thinking out loud."

"Well think in your head and think fucking quicker. The queues are red and that fat cunt Jerome be over now."

I stayed sitting there just looking at the screen still talking to myself a bit but now keeping my voice lower, "he must be back for the cash, he pissed it all away, obviously needs a top up?"

Even though the champ was disrespecting boxing I actually respected the ego of the guy. To be out of the ring for two years, getting up to fuck knows what, and blowing all your cash. To then turn around and say, "Fuck it I'll just have a fight, get a shitload of cash and keep the party going."

Blow all your cash partying, fuck it I'll have a fight keep the party going. Party for a year or so. Blow all your cash, fuck it I'll have a fight keep the party going. Party for a year or so. Blow all your cash, fuck it I'll have a fight keep the party going…..On and on, a vicious circle, literally, until age finally turns around and says, "Fuck You, I ain't doing this anymore." It's no way to build a pension but it'll provide plenty of stories for the grandkids a few years down the line. Like an old wild west gunslinger, drunkenly partying his way through each town taking out the competition along the way for reputation and prize money. But in every walk of life at some point we will all lose to someone who is not as good as us. It's these ones that hurt as we know, we beat ourselves.

In the two years since the champ's retirement the young pup had racked up five straight wins against top 20 world ranked opponents, three of those five against top 10 fighters. He was younger, fitter, healthier and more importantly, hungrier. My mind was made up, I was betting on the pup by KO. I wasn't going to share my information with anyone as I knew some idiot would share it on social media and I'd be in the shit and out of a job. I'm pretty sure it's illegal as well, like insider trading but fuck it, I never turned down a free tip.

When I got home that night, I checked the odds. The champ was 1/3 with the bookies and pup was a stunning 17/5. For a high-profile boxing match these were great odds for the pup, but I wanted more. Pup wasn't a single punch knockout guy; he'd just wear you down until the ref finally said enough's enough and show some mercy. The champ was far more exciting with a long history of stunning Hollywood one punch knockouts on his record. I felt the champ was there for the taking and I was going all in on a KO/stoppage win for the pup, 9/1. But I wanted more. The champ, I believed, would get knocked out by his own lack of preparation as much as by pups fists. How much gas you got in the tank champ? How many rounds can you go? 6? 7? Can you go 10 rounds champ??? For 33/1??? I fucking hope you can champ. I couldn't really afford to lose much but my philosophy in life at that time was I started with nothing and I still got most of it, so fuck it! I believed in signs and I'd missed a bet in 1998 that still haunted me years later. I'd rather now lay the bet and lose. I was prepared to lose cash just to scratch my curiosity and not have another bet follow me around for the next 12 years.

I had Karley coming round for the fight and I knew it was a guarantee I would fuck her. The signs were good so I banged £50 on it.

£50 @ 33/1 gave me a return of £1650.

Don't let me down pup but more importantly, CHAMP don't let me down! Go and train hard enough to last 10-12 rounds and then lie down. Don't go doing something stupid though, like training to win, I don't want you to win, I want you to be stopped or knocked out in round 10, 11 or 12. Then we good champ you can retire then, we'll be good then champ.

Chapter 17

Karley turned up at 7pm on the night of the fight, I was already six cans deep into my Saturday night. I'd got loads of food and alcohol and everything was set for a cozy party for two. She wore a loose fitting mini skirt that skipped around the top of her gym bunny thighs. It was the first time I'd seen the flesh of her legs any higher than the knees before. My dirty mind was racing with all the things I'd like to do to her. Karley's cheeky smile made me know she could read my mind as well. The skirt was accompanied by some white Jordan hi-tops, a fitted t-shirt, denim jacket and curves in all the right places. By 8pm we'd finished two bottles of wine and a few cans. By 8:05 I had Karley bent over my kitchen sink holding on to the taps while I lived the pornstar dream. By 8:10 we'd opened the 3rd bottle of wine. By 8:20 Karley was back over the sink. I didn't have a big cock and I didn't think I was particularly good at fucking, but I was eager and energetic. Always horny, and having a mind dirtier than a shithouse rat enabled me to be a good day and nights company for a woman looking to blow off some steam. We had a great couple of hours before the fighters started their ring walks for the big one. We were both well pissed and looking forward to this.

The champ looked in fantastic shape, he was cut to ribbons and looked confident. Pup was in great shape as well, looking equally confident. Mrs Thedig had told me the champ often rolled his neck excessively when he was nervous or apprehensive. Normally when he had his pants round his ankles by the sound of it. With the drinking, gambling and alleged womanizing, I'd imagine the champ had one of the strongest necks in the world! Karley was buzzing and the thrill of the violence was turning her on. A particularly brutal undercard fight had her on top of me riding away with her skirt around her waist. She had no inhibitions and took pleasure in giving pleasure. Her fiancée was a fucking nerd.

He'd rather play with his Xbox than her box, was how she put it. "Lucky to get fucked twice a month." However, Karley was a different persona to me. Where Karley was the weekend party girl, she was also career driven and wouldn't have liked living my lifestyle. She knew that and so did I, therefore a serious relationship between us was never discussed, as it would have never worked.

ROUND 1 – The champ looks good, he's a bit nervous but he's up on his toes and doing the basics right. Pup's on his toes as well, circling menacingly but other than a few jabs and feints nothing in this round.

ROUND 2 – He's down! The champs down! "For fuck sakes champ not yet, you haven't even gone to rounds. I got fucking 50 quid on you champ, get the fuck up."
The champs up but he's on unsteady legs as he heads back to the corner to end the round.

ROUND 3 – What the fuck!!! Pups down! And he's gone down heavy. His eyes are swimming like an 18-year-old downing their first top shelf, he's fucked!!! The ref's gonna stop this but pup's a tough kid. He calls pup forward and checks his gloves and then waves them together to fight. HE'S DOWN! He's fucking down. The champs gone down again! The excitement is too much for Karley as she dives for my crotch. The champ survives the round.
The bell rings to end the round. The champs bell got rung good and proper, while my bell is getting serviced by a Nymph addicted boxing KO's. Great round.

ROUND 4 – Nobody gets knocked out. Karley's still going.

ROUND 5 – Same

ROUND 6 – Karley blow's my mind and quickly enters my mythical 'top five fucks'.

ROUND 7 – Snacks

ROUND 8 – The fight has gone quiet but I suddenly remember my bet. Karley's welcomed interruption had made me temporarily forget I had money riding on this. The champs probably winning from what I've seen but it's close and the champ looks fucked.

ROUND 9 – Hard right hand from pup, the champ walked on to that. He's down and he's hurt. He's flat out on his back and he's fucked. "No champ! Get up champ, get the fuck up. We need you for another round champ, one more round champ. C'mon champ get up, dig in champ, dig in." On and on I pestered the champ to rise and win me money and he heard my calls. "He's up ref, he's alright, let him fight ref, look at him he wants to fight." Ohh no, no no the doctors on the ring apron, this doesn't look good. It could be stopped. "Please doc, he's alright, couple of stitches, let him fight."
He's ok! The doc says he's ok. "Thanks doc I owe you a drink, c'mon champ get to the end of this round and I'll owe you a fucking barrel." I, unlike most of the viewers, know what lifestyle the champ has really had for the last 6 months thanks to Mrs Thedig. Personally I'm surprised he's got this far, so already it's a great achievement for him. "Last 60 seconds champ, cover up, move off the ropes, watch his right champ, WATCH HIS FUCKING RIGHT HAND YOU DEAF CUNT!!! Get your fucking hands up champ. Last 20 seconds champ, keep moving, stay on your toes, last 10 champ."

DING DING DING. Round 9 ends and the champ is still in the fight. "You've done it champ, you've done it. You've done yourself and everyone else proud champ. Mrs Thedig is so happy champ, I can see her smiling champ. Now, go and lie down for me champ, you deserve it champ you've fought well. Go and lie down for Mrs Thedig champ, she loves you. Lie down for me champ.'' Karley is in stitches laughing at my soliloquy to the champ as we wait for the start of the next round.

ROUND 10 – The bells ring to start the round and both fighters are waved together to continue where they left off. The champ still looks fucked and a punch hasn't been thrown in this round yet as the ref shouts at the time keeper to stop the clock while he looks at the champ.
IT'S OVER, IT'S OVER!!! The champ has been stopped on his feet in the tenth round. It's a perfect ending for me as I'm £1650 richer and I'm happy the champ didn't take anymore punishment. Thanks champ.

I suck up all the positive energy in the room and I'm buzzing. I feel really alive. Yes I'm drunk, but the buzz of the fight and the winnings has sobered me up. As the energy flush slowly subsides back down my body, I get the familiar pins and needles sensation all over my face, all over my body.
"Fancy going out babe? I've got a shit load of winnings, we can grab a couple of grams, go to the casino, get a room somewhere. Get fucked up?'' I looked over but Karley was asleep. KO'd!
It was a warm night but I put a blanket over her anyway. I wrote a note and left it on the coffee table telling her I'd gone to the off licence to buy more drink and I'd be back soon. I went upstairs to wash my dick and change my jeans, then I phoned a dealer named Cozzie and got him to drop me off 3 grams of pure and a lift to town for an extra 10 spot.

I got home at 7:07 in the morning and it was light outside. As I enter the house quietly, I can see Karley is still asleep and the note hasn't been read yet. I don't need to wash my dick again. The 3g of pure I've sniffed made me want to chat to people and have a good time with the drink and music rather than fuck. The £1650 is now £917, with the casino and the drug dealers splitting the rest, along with a couple of impressive bar tabs. Winnings came rarely, and lasted even less, but the sweet ones stay with you. I open an ice cold can of Strongbow from the fridge and I gulp down thirsty mouthfuls until it's empty. I then grab two more before heading to the living room to offer Karley one for help with the hangover. Karley doesn't need any help. We're at it again.

Chapter 18

The weeks in the call centre had moved slowly like the seasons, but the months had quickly rolled into years. I'd turned 30 and I was at the same level in life that I was 21, only a little drunker with a lot less career options to pursue. I wasn't overly bothered about a successful career; I just hated my job. It was decent pay and it was a job I could do stood on my head. Turns out all I had to actually do was sit on my arse. It was a doddle and I could do the job drunk, and I often did. And occasionally high. One Sunday morning after a New Year's party consisting of alcohol and lots of Tramadol, I arranged a £30,000 overdraft for a customer. Considering I was now lending trained that was ok. Considering I couldn't even see my fucking screen to read out all the wording, it probably wasn't ok, but the customer went away happy. I'd think of a valid reason to call in sick every Monday morning but I'd mostly push on through to save the sickies for the real bad hangovers I knew were always around the corner. It was always a risk. You never knew when you would get 'that' call on a Monday. 'That' call, from an angry customer who's spent all weekend writing a fucking speech just to let it rip at some poor hangover pissed up cunt on the other end of the line. Me. The call that made you wish you called in sick.

BEEEEEEEP...LOCKED SECURITY.
First call of the fucking week and it's locked security. I'm hanging out my arse and now I have to run this bozo through a string of fucking

security questions, great. Ok, customers name on screen, here we go, WHAT THE FUCK? No way! No fucking way. Mrs Whore? Mrs fucking Whore on locked security at 8am on a Monday morning? Some fuckers having a laugh here, c'mon. Mrs Whore? Are you fucking serious??? I make a split second decision and dive right in. "Good morning Mrs WhooRay, you're through to Tennyson. How can I help you today?" With one eye closed and slightly ducking down in my seat I wait for Mrs Whore's response to my pathetic attempt to disguise her name. "Grow up young man, say my name as I would. Mrs Whore," came the sharp and bitter bite of an upper-class English toff. Then, to make matters even worse Mrs Whore began to spell her name out. I could see her fucking name on my screen I didn't need it spelled out, but I thought it best if I just kept my mouth shut and listened.

"W for Whiskey, H for Hotel, OOOOO for Oscar, RRRrrr for Romeo and EEEEEeeee for Echoooo." She was Mrs Whore indeed, the spelling it of it confirmed.
"The connotations the words are used for young man are ghastly and I'm well aware. So please take your mind out of the gutter and provide me with some customer service that your tin pot automated machine couldn't."
I wasn't about to get into an argument with Mrs Whore while hungover on a Monday morning with Jerome sleezing behind my back to the young girls on the team, fucking creep. I decided, fuck it, nothing else to do. Just eat shit. And so I did.
"I'm sorry Mrs Whore. It was unprofessional of me and I sincerely apologize for my actions." I was being a little sincere but most of it was just bullshit to avoid getting in an argument.
"That's ok young man, I understand your predicament. I apologize if I barked at you, it was uncalled for."

I was shocked, as I could hear it was a genuine apology, which I quickly accepted and moved on with good grace. I think she found my Welsh accent non-threatening, and she opened up to me about her time in Cardiff University back in the 1970s. Mrs Whore said she still supported the Welsh rugby team to this day after getting hooked on the buzz of the way the team of the 70s played the game. She talked of having a crush on the legendary number 15, JPR. She spoke of his long hair and lamb chop sideburns, and how he looked like Royalty in his blazing red shirt and socks around his ankles. The real Prince of Wales. I started to get visions of JPR smashing Mrs Whore's back doors in on the 22 metre line in front of 80,000 drunk and singing rugby fans. My head was absolutely fried as I just sat there and burst into laughter, right down the fucking phone. Luckily, so did Mrs Whore. The rest of the call went well and after a few more minutes of good natured conversation Mrs Whore and myself ended our conversation.

I suddenly wasn't feeling as bad as I was 10 minutes ago, and then Jerome opened his mouth.
"See United on the weekend Wilde? Best team in Europe, let me fucking tell you." Jerome had lost interest in the girls as they were wise to his sleeze bag shit and could smell the rat on him a mile off. Plus they knew his wife Starr and what a lovely woman she was. A woman who put up with all his shit. Namely sleeping with half her so called 'friends' behind her back. If he wasn't sleazing, he was talking about Manchester United. I bit back.

"Best team in Europe? You fucking drew 1-1 with Burnley at Old Trafford. How the fuck does that result make Man Utd the best team in Europe? They not even the best team in Manchester, let alone fucking Europe Jerome."

My love of football had quickly disappeared after the buzz of the terraces ended when I joined the Navy. Unless I had money on the game, or there was an excuse for an extended drinking session, I couldn't have given a fuck about football anymore. Jerome sulked off to another team to try and sniff around the young girls there. As long as he stayed away from me, I'd be happy. We didn't see the fake tanned, saggy titted, orange face fucktard for the rest of the day. Maybe it's a coincidence, but the rest of the day went well, for a Monday I should have called in sick for.

Chapter 19

When you make a good decision that has a big and positive impact on your life, give yourself credit for that decision. Luck will always be involved but the luck wouldn't have been called upon if the first step hadn't been taken. In the same token, when you make a bad decision that fucks up your life, own that shit too. Take responsibility for that decision and learn from it. Again, luck will have played a part in the scenario but again luck wouldn't have meant a thing if the decision was never made.

After spending all day listening to the new ethos of the bank, I couldn't be fucked staying until 10pm tonight. I cleared it with Leighton to finish early and go to the pub at 6pm. I was sick of hearing the new corporate bullshit phrases "let your behaviours shine so you can influence other people" or my favourite, "promote your brand". They encouraged us to big ourselves up, to give ourselves a pat on the back for the most mediocre shit that was standard to the job we were getting paid to do. The bank had put us in direct competition with each other and it was a dog eat dog office for the bonuses. We were literally battling the person sat next to us for a bigger share of the bonus pot. Grassing, ratting, snitching, whatever you wanted to call it, it was encouraged. People were literally turning on people that they had known for years, people they had introduced to, and in some cases, made part of their families. Shit on! For a few hundred quid, I couldn't be fucked with that.

The job was a game, a game I was really fucking good at. My sales record soared high above the majority of people in the centre. But it wasn't what the bank wanted anymore. CORRECTION. It's what the bank were not allowed to do anymore by law and regulations, certainly not by choice. They still wanted us to sell the same amount as before, but not the hard sell, and also for products now interest rated up the arse as the good times were over.

We had 'targets' to hit even though the 'targets' were nonexistent and actually outlawed.

"Boss why have we got targets?"

"You haven't got targets Tennyson."

"I've just been told I haven't met my monthly targets boss."

"Well Tennyson, that means you're underperforming."

"But we haven't got targets boss?"

"You do not have targets Tennyson, you have behaviour reporting."

"So if I don't hit my behaviour target by selling, I'm underperforming?"

"If you do not display the behaviours we expect you will be underperforming."

"So selling is actually a behaviour expected of us and not a target to meet?"

"That is correct Tennyson, it is part of your job description, therefore failure to achieve this means you're underperforming."

"So to achieve a performing rating I need to sell a certain amount of lending products?"

"Yes Tennyson."

"So in that case, we have a selling target to meet?"

"No, that is not the case."

"So if I sell zero products I will still hit target?"

"There are no targets Tennyson, only behaviours. If you fail to fulfil the requirements of your job role, you will be deemed as underperforming."

"So selling is still part of the job but we can't be seen to reward employees to do this, so we punish them to sell instead, by making an invisible target and name it something else?"
"There aren't any targets Tennyson"

On and on this would go until it became ridiculous to everyone involved. No targets but if you don't hit that target, you're fucked! It was crazy, this was happening in full view of everyone, including the union reps and still nothing was done. The already toxic environment became ten times worse once we started getting rewarded for back stabbing. people were lining up to stick the knife in. I'd spent six years in the Royal Navy where rule one is to look out for your oppo, your shipmate. Not to shit on them at every opportunity and get rewarded for it. Jerome came over and told us all that his bonus still depended on our performances, which we're now behaviour based and not tracked. We would need to log these behaviours ourselves and also provide evidence of this from someone superior. In essence, we came up with behaviours we thought were important, told a manager. Then ask them if it's ok we use them as a witness for our amazing brand of good behaviour, in order to tell everyone how well we are performing. Fucking dickheads.

Jerome was a king rat where backstabbing and snitching were part of his daily routine. He actually enjoyed it and would often gloat about getting someone fired by dropping them in the shit. He turned to me knowing my thoughts about this new system of measuring our performances and my personal thoughts to him as a person as well.
"Wilde. We need big performances from dinosaurs like you,"
 he was fucking older than me the prick.
"Forget those dodgy re-gens with the rest of your dodgy bookkeepers, those days are over. We need behaviours. We need our shit to not stink. We need to be the police on the phones to the customers, and in

the breakroom with your workmates." Jerome was corporate as fuck, one of the many reasons I didn't like him.

"You gonna play ball Wilde and get me my good bonuses? Or are we gonna have to look to manage you out of the place?"

I responded to Jerome as truthfully as I could without being an obnoxious prick like him.

"I give my best to my customers everyday Jerome. Whether I like them or not, I try my best on the call to that customer. If I'm sober or drunk, I will do my best. I'm a customer too and I hate calling the fucking bank, I can empathise with my customers. But I'm not snitching on anyone in work. That's not on my job description Jerome, I'm customer services not the fucking CIA."

Jerome went into a full corporate meltdown of all the buzz words and banking bullshit spill out of his ventriloquist doll's mouth while having the big hard cock of the banking world rammed up his arse. He didn't even have a clue what he was talking about. The fucking imbecile was even making up words to sound dynamic, but just ended up looking like a cunt.

"It's not backstabbing or snitching Wilde, you're not in the military now." I wasn't overly angry or pissed off, I just couldn't keep my big mouth shut.

"Promote your brand Wilde."

I should have just kept left it but it was a catchphrase they had been using all fucking day and it was really bugging me now. And coming out of this shithead's mouth made it even worse.

"Promote my brand? My brand of what? Shit? That's what some cunts are promoting here. I go into the toilets everyday and someone's promoting their brand of shit on the shithouse walls. There was a stickman drawn in shit on the wall yesterday for fuck sakes." Jerome was getting irritated now.

"Yeah I read the email about the toilets Wilde, what's that got to do with your behaviours?"

"Nothing really Jerome. I just don't want to promote my brand in a place that rewards being a snitch. A place I can lose my bonus because a jobsworth has grassed me up for something petty. A place where that same jobsworth, only five minutes ago, was in the toilets with his fingers up his shitty arse drawing fucking stickmen on the wall. I had to take a piss earlier on, with a smiley face of shit looking directly in my eyes. Some cunt had had a game of noughts and crosses with himself the other day."

The subject was quickly changed by Jerome who was uncomfortable in being challenged like this in front of the staff he was so used to bullying. Well he was a bully, and I didn't fucking like him. Yeah he could fire me if he wanted, I knew that. He also knew that out of work I could easily bump into him at the gym we both used and give him a fucking slap.

"Just do your job Wilde. That's why you're still on the phones in your 30s with no ambition. Your attitude stinks." And he walked off.
"Yeah it stinks, like the shit smeared toilet walls, I'm just trying to blend in. I might stick my fingers up my arse later and promote my brand."
Jerome didn't turn back even after I called him a prick loud enough for him and everyone else on the team to hear.
"Ten! Pack it in boy," Leighton had chipped in knowing that my giving Jerome shit would now come down on his head.
"I'm sorry Late, but he's a fucking arse bandit mate."
"He'll have it in for us all now Ten, starting with me."
"Fuck him," I'd already done the red rag to a bull stuff and was getting angry and obnoxious now.
"Look Ten, just get back on the phones and you're out of here in an hour with a pint in your hand."

That did calm me a bit and give me something to look forward to. I didn't like wasting holiday hours on half day finishes but I'd had enough today. I'd walk to the pub and get drunk to cheer myself up. I could have taken 3 hours, 4 hours, 5 or 6. I chose 4 hours as I didn't have the cash for 6 hours in the pub tonight. I'd made a decision. It'd be nice if that decision was blessed with a little luck, I certainly could do with some. I put my headset back on for the last hour and clock watched until 6pm which felt like an eternity. I packed up my stuff and got the fuck out of there before they changed their minds, which had happened before. Promote your brand, yeah right. Fuck your brand.

Chapter 20

The monotonous late night walks home in the dark rarely offered any entertainment value, unless I'd managed to win some booze from work which was now hardly ever. As I walked my usual path by the riverside at my earlier than usual time, I took in the natural beauty. The things I took for granted on the hungover return journeys I would take the next mornings. It was 6:10pm and the sun was still shining bright. I'd removed my jacket and the shirt underneath clung to my sweaty body but the gentle breeze was refreshing against my chest. In the distance I could see a silhouette, the silhouette of a woman. But the sun was too bright as I squinted into the distance. My eyes narrowed until they were almost closed and all I could see was her silhouette and the white light around it. In a moment of silence the breeze dropped to almost nothing and my vision became playful and unpredictable as I saw a lightning strike of a rainbow flash crash through the kaleidoscope scenes of my kaleidoscope dreams. Her name was Genevieve.

Genevieve had moon shadow black hair which danced around her shoulders as the gentle breeze returned. She wore gym clothes that hugged her shapely figure. Wasp waisted but both her breasts and bum were firm and plentiful. The sun started to clear from my eyes and all the colour came back to my vision instead of the painful bright white light I'd fought through. Looking in her early 20s Genevieve raised her hand to her mouth as she giggled at my blushing face as I slowly walked past. We shared a friendly smile and I was transfixed by her deadly blue eyes that were portraying both danger and desire in equal measure. Her eyes didn't so much suck you in, they sort of grabbed you by the throat and punched you in the face. After meeting Genevieve I immediately felt ugly.

"Sweating a bit there mister?"
Ahh for fuck sakes, a traveller. I was on guard straight away. A situation I had got myself into bed with a few years previously had ended up being a situation of me taking a beating off an angry husband and the two brothers of his traveller bride. It was a well deserved beating and I had no complaints. I had a broken nose and 12 stitches through my eyebrow, but no complaints.

"Hahaha, yeah it's a hot day, I've taken off what I can without getting arrested for indecent exposure," I flirted even though I knew it was trouble. "It's a hot day and a pretty girl raised my temperature so I'm going for a cold beer. You coming?" Fucking idiot. I didn't even mean to say that. I was slowly walking backwards, away from the temptation that would 99% get me a fucking kicking, and I had to open my fucking mouth. "Yeah ok mister, the sun's hot and I've done my workout, let's go." I almost trip on my ass while doing the 180 degrees turn back into my walking stride, as my invitation is accepted. We walk to the pub.

Most relationships I had been in had started in similar ways, by me being a confident, cocky, arrogant fuck. That actually, was totally against my true character but by this stage in my life I had forgotten what my true character was and relied on alcohol to emotionally dress me each day. My alcohol suit of armour prevented anyone from seeing the real damaged goods. I was just a caricature of lost little boy in a man's body. A quick ass and interesting company when drunk led me into many doomed to fail, party time relationships. The relationships normally faded out as quickly as the parties that initially spawned them. As Genevieve and I walked the leafy riverside path the conversation flowed freely and easily. I'd learned that Genevieve was 22 years old, a free spirit, and all I'd ever desired in a woman. We sat in the beer garden of my local pub undisturbed, apart from the occasional pub regular walking passed giving their best regards. We had a great couple of hours getting to know each other in the sunshine, where Genevieve impressively matched me drink for drink. I don't know if it was the drink or maybe she just felt at ease around me but Genevieve really opened up to me.

She told me that she was engaged to get married to a man from the traveller community. He was over in Ireland. Genevieve said he didn't travel outside of Ireland unless it was an absolute emergency anymore. A previous trip had resulted in him having to be smuggled back into Ireland for fear of a lengthy prison sentence, going into double figures, according to Genevieve. He was older than Genevieve. He was even older than my 31-year-old drunk ass. Tall and fat, I was told he had the definition of a jellyfish. But a jellyfish with a nasty sting and even nastier friends. I felt sorry for Genevieve. I felt like she was trapped. But she wasn't. Genevieve loved her roots and loved the traveller community. She just didn't love the man she was due to marry. Genevieve would remark about my muscular physique and slim body as the talk got looser and dirtier as the drinks continued to flow while the sun started to disappear behind a nearby church.

"Ten, can we go back to your house please? I'm feeling cold."
We'd shared some pretty deep shit over the last few hours and it felt like we had known each other for years. During our conversation the

question of where I lived had come up. By coincidence I lived less than 500 yards from the pub.

"Of course babe, we'll go back and chat some more. Don't try any funny business though. Just cos I'm a sailor doesn't mean I'm easy."
I was in full swing. Laughing and cracking jokes like the class clown, I could see Genevieve liked me for me. She liked my stories and she liked a drink but she didn't like the way I drank when I told her this was a daily thing for me. Genevieve didn't like nose candy either. Her father had died an alcoholic and also many of her childhood friends had got under the wing of the drink and the powered white lady. She told me how coke had got into the traveller community and caused havoc. Men and women she had known for years, turned into monsters in front of her eyes. We walked the road home and arrived at 20:57, it was still early.

I unlock the front door and we both stumble inside as I turn and fumble to put the security chain on. Years of paranoia issues along with a long list of law-breaking acquaintances had made me security conscious. As I turn to Genevieve, she wraps both her arms around me and kisses me passionately. We drag each other up the stairs, ripping off bits of clothing as we go. Drunkenly giving in to the sexual chemistry present even though we both know it's not a good idea. The pull is too strong. There was no time for foreplay as Genevieve stripped me naked and demanded I fuck her. These were Genevieve's words, not mine, but I happily obliged. It was frantic, hot, intense, mind blowing, but ultimately, rushed. The ultimate quicky, as we both fucked each other's brains out and I come deep inside Genevieve. We collapse into each other's arms and spend the rest of the evening making love. Alcohol doesn't even cross my mind and I haven't spoken to the voices of the apocalypse tonight which is normally guaranteed when I'm half shitfaced. I feel like I have made a connection and I wake up in the morning genuinely looking forward to seeing this person again. This feeling is new to me and I feel like I could run with it.

Chapter 21

I walked home the same route every night. Whether it was the early or late shift, Genevieve would be waiting for me on our riverside path. We sometimes made love on the sheltered riverbank during the darker late shifts but most of the time we would take the 10-minute walk back to my house. We spend hours learning about each other and each other's troubled histories. It wasn't just about the sex but that was amazing for both of us as well. It was new each time and never failed to get the blood flowing. I could bring Genevieve to climax just by the touch of my fingertips over her body, she was so sensitive to my touch, penetration wasn't always required but inevitably that's how it always ended up. We were caught up in the moment and didn't care for the consequences. It was animalistic. Genevieve told me she loved me. She told me her mother knew about us and knew Genevieve was in love with a man who was not her fiancée.

"Are you fucking nuts babe? I'm gonna get fucking murdered if your clan finds out about me!"
Genevieve looked at me disgustingly that I could suggest such a thing from her family. She had conveniently forgotten that she had a psychopath future husband waiting for her in Ireland who was staring down the barrel of a double digit prison sentence.
"I had to tell someone babe. Me and my mum are so close she already knew, she could sense it. I couldn't keep it from here any longer, I love you Ten."
I was shying away from dropping the L bomb myself so I changed the subject back to the mother issue.
"So, what did she say? Did she go mental? Did she kick off?"

"No baby, she understands but she says it can't last forever. I will have to go back to Ireland at the end of the summer to get married. I don't want to get married to him Ten, I don't ever want to marry someone who's not you. My sweet Genevieve was now crying and shaking, having what I now know to be a panic attack. I didn't know what to do so I hugged her and reassured her. I told Genevieve I loved her, and I meant it. This made her cry even more as we hugged each other's naked bodies to sleep.

I would walk passed Genevieve's traveller site everyday but I would never see her. We were careful to not get spotted flirting or talking, especially as Genevieve's mother now knew the full story. I knew the travellers would eventually pack up and move on, that's what travellers do. I'd been seeing Genevieve for five weeks already and it was only the start of June. We had months until she had to leave for Ireland. Due to a medical condition Genevieve had, she would only ever be able to have one child. This caused problems with potential partners in the traveller community as Genevieve would talk about the traditional big families and how important it was to have brothers and sisters. An only child in the traveller community would cause the child to be alienated and looked down on, along with Genevieve.

When Genevieve's father died one of his friends became a father figure to her. Over the years the relationship intensified and Genevieve became trapped in a relationship with a man she didn't love who was well over 20 years older than her. He already had a grown up family but wanted to pop a final kid out with Genevieve. That would be it, that would be Genevieve's one and only shot. When we met that night we both tried to look for the positives. "We've still got 3 months until you have to go back to Ireland babe, let's try and enjoy our time together." My empty words didn't even convince me. I'd only been drunk 5 or 6 times in 5 or 6 weeks since I met Genevieve. That was unheard of and I was in shock when it dawned on me. I was looking a bit healthier and my mental health had dramatically improved over the weeks with Genevieve in my life. I felt good. No. I felt fucking great. I had no ties and a fucking job I hated that I would happily bin off in a heartbeat. I would have run away with Genevieve that day if she had asked me. I tell Genevieve this and she cries. She hugs me with both arms and she tells me she loves me. Genevieve tells me she will not return to Ireland, she is ready to cut her ties, we will travel the world together and be the free spirits we were born to be. Money is not a concern as Genevieve was left a large inheritance by her dad along with property and loads of expensive shit. She goes on to tell me that we could afford to travel the world for a few years before settling down into a fully paid property wherever we liked. Genevieve wanted to get me better and was the first person to recognise that the alcohol wasn't my problem, I was my own problem. She could tell a chronic alcoholic when one was put in front of her, she'd watched her beloved father drink himself to death in front of her eyes, barely out of his 30s. I had no idea about Genevieve's wealth when I fell in love with her. I wanted Genevieve because I loved her, not for her money. I was born with nothing and I still had most of it. I'd never had real love.

"You can't tell your mum babe; you know that right?"
"I know that Ten, I won't tell her babe. I'll write her a letter once we leave. She'll be understanding, she knows how I feel about you."

Genevieve was calm and happy once we had made our decision. I could tell that she had been thinking about this for a while, I was glad Genevieve was happy. She was always happy now. Even though my drinking had reduced dramatically, I was still drinking everyday. I would get drunk on the weekends and then keep the engine ticking over for the rest of the week with a few nightly cans to ward away the night terrors. It wasn't perfect but it was a positive step. It was nice waking up without a hangover and feeling good. More importantly, feeling good about my life and future for the first time in my adult life but

Genevieve could see the roots of my drinking problem were long, strong and complicated.

"Babe, you know you have a drinking problem right? I'm not having a go at you, I want to support you. I watched my father drink himself to death, I can't watch the only other man I've ever loved do the same thing. I'll never leave you Tennyson but it will make me sad to see you punish yourself. I don't want you to die." Ahhh man, the deep shit. The drinking, that bus is never fucking late. I didn't even kick off anymore as I was, by this point, well aware of my alcoholism. I was also aware of my ferocious temper and how drink fueled it. For years I would wake up in the morning and check my fists to see if they offered any hint about what had happened the night before. How the fuck I wasn't in jail I don't know. The only problem I had, is that I didn't give a fuck. I didn't care about myself or others. Alcohol wasn't my problem. Alcohol was my symptom. I was my problem. I was robbing myself of a life. I was robbing my soul with every drink I took and I enjoyed the feeling of being in a position to say 'fuck it.' As far as I was concerned alcohol enhanced my life and I had no desire to quit. I loved Genevieve but I could survive without her. I didn't love alcohol but I knew I couldn't live without it, I wasn't ready.

I once saw a mentally ill crow when I was 10 years old. It followed my friend around, it thought he was it's mother. Was alcohol my crow??? I think maybe I was the crow.
"Yeah babe, I know I drink too much. It's a South Wales thing babe, I been drinking since I was 8." Genevieve looked shocked but also really sad and upset as she knew I was being totally truthful.
"Ten that's terrible, that's not normal behaviour babe. I don't care where you grow up, drinking that young is not normal."

My mam and dad never knew I drank when I was that young, it would be by my mid-teens before my drinking was a visible problem. I found my own path and got lost all by myself. They were both good people and good parents who tried their best with me. All the responsibilities of wrong decisions I've made over the years rested with me; my parents are innocent. I knew it was wrong even when I was that young but I still couldn't help myself. Most of the time it was just mine sweeping left over drinks from the bar tables that people had forgotten about or taken their eye off while I searched around for 20 pence for a game of pool. The pub was my youth club. I was obviously too young at the time to realise that indulging in this new hobby while rolling solo was the first sign I was an alcoholic. Even before a single pube had sprouted around my little dick I was a budding alcoholic in training and a good little thief too. Nobody was safe from my thirst and I would target stores that didn't have the alcohol kept by the tills to steal from. Sometimes I would drink the cans straight off the shelf and then put them back before staggering out of the shop drunk as fuck at 10 years old. I was fucking wild and the poster child for the argument that alcoholics are born, not made. Alcoholics will naturally find their way to booze at some point in their lives. I just found my destiny earlier than most.

"The goal is to be sober by 40 babe, completely tee total, that's the plan. Get to like 39, then start cutting down. By my 40th birthday I'll almost be sober. We'll go out and celebrate, get fucking hammered, get loads of coke, get right off our tits. Go into my 40s in style." Genevieve wasn't convinced. "No Ten. Go into your 40s still alive. My dad got to 41 but in reality, he actually died in his 30s. He'd given up hope. He'd given up on the prospect of a sober life. He committed suicide, slowly and painfully." I could see a lot of similarities between myself and Genevieve's father, we would have probably got on.

"Well I've got my plans babe. I hit my targets in work, I turned 32 last week, I've got a beautiful girlfriend and a happy future ahead. We'll be gone by September and I'll be sober before I'm 40. I've got targets babe. I'm a target hitting motherfucker. And I'm good looking as fuck." I had a grin on my face from ear to ear or a cocky smirk as Genevieve likes to call it.

"Listen to you ya big headed fucker. If you're that good looking try sucking your own cock, let me know how that goes for you my handsome boy." We both burst into laughter, the banter was always fresh and funny with Genevieve. I wasn't a bad looking guy but nowhere near where my confidence was. For someone who hated themselves as much as I did, I certainly didn't lack in confidence. Genevieve once remarked that I was like every bad guy she'd seen in the movies. The guy we shouldn't like but can't help it. She told me I was every bad guy rolled into one body, smothered with confidence and a pretty face, smacked on the ass and sent out into the world to cause chaos. I was her drug; she couldn't get enough of me and I was the only drug she ever needed or wanted. Genevieve was my drug too, but only one of them. There were others I wanted and needed to help me function my train wreck of a life. Not other women, actual drugs, I needed them. I was a functioning alcoholic, paranoid schizophrenic and borderline drug addict. I needed the routine of anarchy to keep the balance in my life. I did also need Genevieve, as we both discovered, no, I can't suck my own cock.

Chapter 22

In work you're targeted on everything, there's no place to hide. Your log on times, break times, lunch times, how many calls you've taken, how many sales, how many customer satisfaction surveys. Everything was measured and compared against your peers. There was also something called AHT, average handling time. The bank wanted each customer to get a maximum of 300 seconds to deal with their issues and get the fuck off the phone for the next sucker to come through. If you're averaging over 300 seconds per call, you're costing the bank money and they will eventually manage you out of the place. This was just brushing the real problem under the rug and punishing the innocent, which in this case was us, the telephone operators. The bank was losing too much money, it couldn't be to do with all the money laundering shit, we were innocent as a bank, but we accepted the billions in fines they handed down, along with all the new banking regulations. We accepted record fines and sanctions but still never apologized or admitted we were in the wrong. I'd never worked for anyone with such little integrity. Instead of the bank taking a long hard look at itself and how much it fucked up because of greed, it instead looks to blame the people it employs at the lowest level. We are the most expendable. There is blood of innocent children, caught up in the drug wars in Mexico that the bank helped launder money for the cartels. The bank never apologized for its actions or even repented. We just looked to do the same things again but not get caught this time. Innocent children were tortured to death just so the banks shareholders could enjoy their annual millions in dividends. Let's take the focus off our relationship with the Mexican drug cartels and instead focus our attention to the thing that will save our bank and restore full faith in us to the general public. We need AHT to be 280 not 300. Do that and it will solve everything. Fucking dickheads.

I was averaging about 240 seconds, it was never a problem for me. Some days when I really couldn't be fucked with the customer service shite I could be down around the 180 mark. Call comes through, what do you want? Done. Anything else? Good, fuck off. Next! I seemed to think the quicker I got the customers off the phone the quicker the clock would spin round. It obviously didn't but it did help me avoid doing the cringey customer service fake ass shit. Fuck that. Just get it done and get the fuck off my phone. While time was passing too quick and I was getting old in the place, the working week dragged like fuck. I wished the time away and I wished the days away. I wished the weeks into oblivion until the concept of time becomes irrelevant and I wonder what is the point in the first place of the thing I'm wishing away. Time gets written off to progress my march towards the weekend drinking marathons. I hated the Monday mornings but a good Monday morning would mean I've had a shit weekend, but I was changing. Wishing for the weekends no longer excited me, I just saw it as wishing for another Monday morning to roll around. It was around this point I had made the decision to make every morning a Monday and just drink every fucking day to nullify it. I didn't know how to live my life but I knew how to keep it consistent, I just needed to stay drunk, permanently. I could avoid the really shit day which was a Monday morning once a week by having shit days every day. Only an alcoholic will truly understand this, not even junkies have the spiritual malady alcoholics do. A junkie will need their regular fix to satisfy their craving, their addiction. A chronic alcoholic's only fix is to drink to blackout, nothing else will suffice. If junkies had the spiritual malady alcoholics do, there would be dead junkies littering the streets of every major city in the world. If an alcoholic's drug of choice was heroin, we would overdose every night.

Every. Single. Night.

No matter how much we drink, the craving is never satisfied. But I had Genevieve now and I didn't want to fuck this up. I also wanted Genevieve to see me as something more than a drunk with loads of jokes and a quick ass. I knew I would eventually drink myself to death, and for over a decade, I was good with that. It wasn't fair for Genevieve to go through this again though.

Due to my AHT being around the 240 mark, the bank, in its wisdom, unleashed me as the AHT champion. I was to help people struggling on the phones to get under 300, then under 280. I was good at this aspect of the job as I knew the boundaries. I wasn't here to be your friend but I was here to be friendly. I was here to service you and sell you shit, and then get you off the fucking phone. Simple. Don't get me wrong, customers service and skills are good. Being nice is important too, it's actually fucking essential, especially in the first 30 seconds of the call where the battle is ultimately won or lost. You can normally determine how 90% of your calls will go within the first 15 seconds. Stamp your influence at this point, at the start, be the boss. Don't match a prick by being a prick, use your fucking brains. If a person's being a prick to you, don't play the person, play the game. What beats a prick??? Pussy! You don't beat a prick by throwing another prick at it, throw some pussy the pricks way. Sit back, listen to the customer, write shit down, pick up inconsistencies in what they say, keep your fucking mouth shut, just listen, keep writing. Once the customer has finished chatting shit, once the customers has made themselves out to be a prick, throw the pussy at them. Take them to the fucking cleaners with all the calm shit you wrote down and listened to, while the prick was being a prick. Take them to a fucking kangaroo court, remind them all calls are recorded, remain calm and polite at all times. Do not raise or lower your voice, keep calm, keep consistent. Pussy beats prick. 240.

That was basically all the training tips I could give to my charges. I just had to rearrange it around each individual I coached. Give them the same message but use a different method of planting it in their minds to grow for future times. The results were amazing. After one week of coaching 20 people individually, 80% had ended up getting under 300. After two weeks the same 20 people were now 100% pass rate but for 280 and not 300. After a month there were over 50 of my trainees taking approximately 20 more calls per day. That may not sound much but over the month that equated to an extra 20,000 calls being taken by the same individuals who had struggled the month before. I'd saved the bank thousands of pounds, high level thousands too, probably not far off the 6 digit thousands. They were servicing more customers, quicker and more efficiently than before. The wage bill dropped as overtime was not required as the queues were taken care of in the working day. The wait times decreased, the customer satisfaction surveys went up as customers were happier with shorter queues and also less fluffy bullshit when they finally got to speak to a rep. And I achieved this by telling my troops that the customer was their enemy, not their friend. The customer was trying to keep them on the phone for over 300 seconds, the fucking cunt. Stop them doing it, don't be their fucking friend, service them and fuck them off. You want to keep that cunt Jerome off your back? Then get your 280, fuck the 300 let's have fun. The customers are trying to get us sacked by keeping us on the phones, get um off, they ain't your fucking mates, they're trying to get you in the shit, trying to get Jerome on your back, they're fucking spies, kill the cunts, kill them by getting 280!!!

That last bit of advice was what I used on Pacman. He was really good at his job but his AHT was shite. He couldn't cut a conversation off when needed, he was too nice. Through hard work, Pacman went from 355 to 315 in less than a week. A week later he was down to 299. By the following month he was down to 282 and he would then break that 280 barrier on numerous occasions thereafter. He didn't need coaching anymore and ended up actually doing the coaching himself for others. I could not have got Pacman down to 280 by telling him to do it the way the bank wanted it done. I had to be me. All I did was show people what I did and how I did it. I went on to coach a lot of other people in the office, female and male using the same Pacman tactics. I had to be careful about my coaching techniques, as I didn't need some cunt whinging that I'd been dropping the C bomb like a motherfucker all day. Jerome and HR hated me so they'd have a field day. I had been picked up before for my colourful use of the English language while coaching. It was only a 'fuck' though. Can get away with loads of fucks but you drop one cunt and it could be curtains. I would have told the cunts to stick the job but I enjoyed the perks of not having to go on the phone, sometimes for weeks on end. If I could avoid just one call a day it was once less potential cocksucker that could ruin it. Ruining of my day was my job, I fucking hated when a customer ruined my day the selfish cunt. I've been doing a wicked job of ruining my days for the last 15 years thank you very much, don't need your help.

I squeezed every second I could out of not having to take calls and I made myself look busy when I was actually doing fuck all. However, my results spoke for themselves and all I did was preach my bad habits, including drinking and drugs, to my trainees. I got the results, fucking good results too. One of my coaching days fell on the day all the managers had gone to an ass licking conference in England. We had the centre to ourselves and I basically spent all day just walking round talking to people about mad shit. I'd chat about football to some of the lads, Tequila shots with some of the young girls, music and movies to any cunt that would listen. I'd have the young girls flirt with me after they'd seen me rucking in town on the weekend. Then Gerald would come over and tell me in front of the girls about how he made me his bitch in his dream last night, which always ended up in a group of us reduced to uncontrollable laughter. It was a decent day in the office.

Pacman was in good spirits too as we ripped into him about his fucking eight names. James Dean Buster Douglas John Dean Jesse Luke Desade. The story behind it sounded like one of my fucked up weekends but it was funny. Pacman's dad had won a shitload of cash on the Mike Tyson v Buster Douglas fight which was held in Tokyo. It made my winnings on the champ look like chump change as Pacman's pops cleared over £100,000 in winnings. I got told later down the line by Old Pacman himself that he betted £3000 on Buster Douglas at 44/1, cleared £132,000. So, in honour of Buster Douglas, Pacman Sr decided to change one of the names from Dean to Douglas. However, when given the responsibility of registering the birth, Pacman Sr turned up still half cut from the weekend partying while Momma Pacman and baby

Pacman were still in hospital. In trying to remember to take the name Dean out and replace it with Douglas, Pacman Sr fucked up royally. Not only did he forget to take Dean out, he actually put it down twice. And instead of Douglas which Momma Pacman agreed, he went full hog and put it as Buster Douglas. The drink and drugs of 1990 melted Poppa Pacman's brain and the job of writing a name on a bit of paper was obviously too fucking much responsibility. Fuck knows what due diligence was going on in the place as the registerer must have been as fucked as Poppa Pacman. Dean was written down twice along with the most famous name on the planet for the whole of 1990 and it still slipped through the net.

On a normal day Pacman would flip out at being called 'Double Dean' and we would laugh like fuck at his fury. Today he joined in, as he told us more stories about the crazy shit Poppa Pacman got up to over the years while drunk and high, and Momma Pacman's equally hilarious reactions. Poppa and Momma Pacman were out in town most weekends and were popular and well known by most regular weekend party heads. I enjoyed their company and always made a point of spending some time with them when I saw them out. I got quite emotional one night when Momma Pac told me how John (Pacman) would talk about me and the positive effect I was having on his confidence. He was a good kid and I was fond of him as I would have been if I ever had a younger brother. He was a good time Charlie on the weekends but still young enough to brush the hangovers off quite easily.

I could see many similarities between Pacman and myself when I was in my mid 20s like he was, but I could see that Pacman was a much better human being than myself. He was just bored and unchallenged not broken and damaged. He was too good for this place as I watched them suck the priceless fountain of youth from his body to eventually turn his soul black. I secretly hoped Pacman would get sacked. He was young and earning good money for a job he could do in his sleep. He had a good lifestyle which he loved and the decent wages enabled that lifestyle to continue. When he would complain about his job and how much he hated it, I would point out all the opportunities outside the bank that were available to a young person like him. It all came back to money though, most of which he would spend on his 'boy racer' car and partying on the weekend. Pacman was comfortable here, too comfortable. He would never jump, Pacman would need to be pushed.

I left Pacman in the capable hands of Sadie and Jess who teased him like two older sisters would and I went for a walk. Mario, who was a young and well liked Polish guy came bouncing over all excitedly.

"Hey Ten, Ten. You know Joanne? Joanne off the Credit card team?"
I did know her and was about to say so when Mario cut me off and continued his story.
"I got date with her Ten. I have been after her for while Ten, fucking year now Ten, my fucking balls are blue for her Ten. But I got date now Ten."
Luckily Mario had interrupted my reply to his question. Yes, I did know Joanne. How??? Well, Glug had been with her last summer, or according to Glug he'd "fucked her retarded for 3 months." It was not something I was overly keen to tell my excited young friend, so I lied.
"I don't know her well Mario, just that she's on the credit card team and a very good looking lady, good personality as well I've heard pal." I was full of shit. I didn't have a fucking clue about her other than what Glug had told us, and all he had told us was she was a dirty bitch who loved the cock.
With perfect timing Sharkhead swims up beside us.
"All right fellas, what's happening?"
Before Shark could finish his greeting, Mario had already blurted out about Joanne.
"I got date with Joanne Shark, you know Joanne off credit cards?"

Turning to look at me with those blank, dark, shark eyes and running his giant sharkhead fucking mouth he looks at me and I know it's coming but I can't say anything. I'm just thinking, 'no Shark, don't do it, think for fuck sakes, don't say it.' Too fucking late.

"Ain't that the one that Glug fucked retarded last year?"

I close my eyes tight and hold in the laughter until it's painful. I open my eyes to see Mario has gone bug eyed to fuck. He's turned pale and grey as his shoulders slouch and he looks completely uncomfortable where he's stood, as if he's just shit his pants.

Mario's lip quivers. "Glug fuck Joanne? Aww no, not Glug, please no Glug. He got that pornstar dick man. Glug get his cock out when we drunk in town. Fucking huge man, aww no, Glug why you fuck Joanne man? Why you have to stick her man?" Both Shark and myself are now feeling terrible as it's obvious this kid is heartbroken.

"Everyone's been with someone else Mario. I was with my brother's wife for 6 months before they knew each other, I shagged her arse raw. It's ok though as I knew her first." Shark's words that had caused the panic attack in the first place were now being used to calm the situation. It seemed to be working. Shark continued.

"Look man, don't worry about Glugs big dick, he don't know how to use the fucker anyway the stoner. He was probably too stoned to get his cock hard mate."

Mario's breathing had slowed down and returned to almost normal, while the colour returned to his face.

"Ok guys, I go. I go on date with Joanne. I go on date with Joanne not with Glug's big dick. Glug big cock not important to me. I go. Thank you Shark, thank you Ten, you are good friends."

Mario bounced off happy, just as he had bounced up, on cloud 9 and loving life. I smiled for the rest of the day and was excited to see Genevieve later that evening. I'd had a key cut for her and I'd also bought an engagement ring. I planned on asking the already engaged gypsy beauty to marry me once we eloped from Wales in September. I had no doubts she would say yes, but I was still nervous.

Chapter 23

I put the engraved house key in an empty ring box I had picked up at the store. I had the engagement ring in its original red velvet box in my back pocket.

The four voices of the apocalypse had made an appearance during champagne shopping so on Dev's insistence we picked up a load of cans too. We talked amongst ourselves and all four of us loved Genevieve. We all loved her for different reasons but it was all love. Dev encouraged me to have a can of lager to calm the nerves even though I wasn't nervous. We had a can anyway. I was confident, the champagne was chilling, the roses and chocolates were ready, bed done all nice. I had no doubts she would say yes.

At about 6pm there was a knock on the door and I could see her raven mane of hair through my frosted glass. "Hey babe, good day? Get the kettle on then." Genevieve was oblivious to the whole set up as she nonchalantly walked past me and straight into the kitchen. I picked up the box with the key in, trying to keep a straight face during the whole childish prank. I hold both her hands and slip the box into her palms. She pulls her hands away and clasps the box in both hands, still not averting her gaze from my eyes. A massive grin glows across her face as she kisses my cheek and says. "Thanks for the key babe, I love it." Winking at me while still holding the unopened box I question here about how she knows? "The weight of the box babe, the key is much heavier than a ring." My planned prank had crashed and burned so I encouraged Genevieve to open the box anyway, all while teasing her that she had inherited her mother's fortune telling powers. The standard house key was unremarkable apart from the engraving 'Genevieve XXX' on the blank side of the key. As she opened the box to reveal the key I placed the other box in her hand as well. "Well if you're having that, you may as well have this too." Handing her the red velvet box I see her speechless for the first time ever. Without opening the box, she begins to cry and tells me it's all she's ever wanted. She tells me I'm all she's ever wanted. Genevieve hugs me close and tells me softly, "Yes babe, I love you and want to spend the rest of my life with you. I want my one child to be with you. I've never wanted anyone else Ten." We kissed passionately as Genevieve led me to the bedroom while the engagement ring stayed in the box on the kitchen side.

Later on, we pulled the ring out and played about with it while we ate chocolates, drank champagne and made love. We both thanked our own creators of destiny. Genevieve's was God, mine was good luck. We decided it was best to leave the ring in my house as it wasn't worth the risk of Genevieve being caught with it. Especially as we only had just over two months before we would escape. I insisted she held on to the key though and just keep it hidden. Her mother knew about me anyway so a key could be explained away quite easily. A £400 engagement ring in a red velvet box may be a bit harder to explain away to a psychic. I didn't fancy our chances so we didn't take any. The ring stayed in the box and it was put with my music collection, the only other possessions I gave a fuck about along with my dog.

Over the next few days we discussed our plans and the places we would travel to. Genevieve was officially the traveller of the partnership but apart from Ireland, Wales and England she'd never actually travelled anywhere. During my time in the Navy I was given an ID card, food and shelter, basic training, trade training, and then on to a ship handsome boy for a worldwide adventure. I was paid a good wage and officially I was a sailor. In terms of reality though, and my true intentions, I was nothing but a pirate hitching a ride. Looking for drink, women and fighting, in no particular order, my only plans were to get drunker than I did the day before.

I had travelled to some wonderful places across the globe but missed out on the 'far east' deployment due to an assault charge I had to face the music for in Portsmouth city centre. Instead of looking at the trip of a lifetime, I was looking at two years in jail. I eventually got found not guilty but I still missed the trip. I felt like Genevieve was a special person, destined for great things. There was an aura about her that convinced me she was her for a special reason, she would leave her mark on the world. I wanted her to make the decisions about where we would go, I just wanted to follow her and see where she went. I wanted to be part of the journey of this incredible person. I wanted to put my life in her hands. I wanted her to have control over something I no longer had any control over, maybe I never did.

I made it my goal in life to love and serve this person forever. Genevieve made me believe there was a better life for me, for us. She encouraged me to love myself and forgive myself of my previous sins that I no longer had any control over. She sobbed sometimes when I told her about my past, she wept that she wasn't there for me. She tells me she'll never leave me. I worship this woman.

The daily walk past her site, by the river, on my way to work always brightened my day even though I wouldn't actually see her. I could feel her watching me from afar. I still hated my job with a passion but I loved Genevieve with a passion much stronger. I could see the end of the tunnel. I can see our escape.

SMS Text message

"I'll be round about 7 babe. I'll cook food tonight then going back to stay with mum. Been out a few nights this week so don't want to push it. Walk me home tonight and I may suck your cock by the river ;-) "
Genevieve, July 21st, 2012

I'd love the cheeky texts I'd get throughout the day; it made the monotony of life bearable. Genevieve came round at 6:47pm and I ended up cooking for her rather than her cook for me. We had a few drinks and made love in bed for an hour or so. At 9:33pm we left my house and made the 10-minute walk back to where her mother's caravan was parked up with the rest. We walked over 'dog shit bridge' and Genevieve laughed as I told her that I had named it that myself. It was a walkway that went over six lanes of busy traffic to reach the river the other side. It was a main walkway for dog walkers, and their dogs who liked to shit all over the bridge. It hit its peak in 2009 when it officially became 'dodge the dogshit bridge' and in 2011 after a move to the night shift it got renamed 'dodge the dogshit in the dark bridge.' We walked to our well used and cozy spot on the river bank. It was a still, warm, July night. We had sex on the river bank as passionately as we ever had, and as passionately as we would tomorrow. I'd seen Genevieve everyday since we first met. "Straight home now naughty boy. No stopping off for a few pints. Home and sleep. I'll keep an eye out for you walking past in the morning, I always do. I love you so much babe, you're my soulmate. It won't be long and we won't have to hide and we'll be together forever."

I had no intention of drinking tonight. It had become something that I was thinking about less and less. I still talked to the voices but it was more about Genevieve rather than drinking. The conversations were positive and as the grip of alcohol loosened its grip on my soul, the conversations became less frequent. I was getting better, slowly, but I was getting better, physically and mentally.

"Ok babe, I'll text you when I'm home. You go over now and I'll watch you from here to make sure you get in all right."

"What! Like some pervert in the bushes in the dark? No wonder our sex life is like it is!!!"Genevieve could always drag the conversation to the gutter, and I could then drown it in the shit infested water where she took it.

"Yeah, I'll stand in the bushes with my cock in my hand hoping to catch a glimpse of your mother!"

"TEN!!! You're disgusting, that's my mum. Stay away from her, she'll fancy you as well, I know what she's like." I gave her a big hug and quick squeeze of the bum before I sent her back over to her mum's caravan as I watched from the darkness. Cock in my pants. I watch her put her hand on the door and turn around. From the darkness of the woods, I step out into the light and blow Genevieve a kiss. As normal she blows one back as I wave and step back into the darkness as Genevieve goes inside and closes the door.

I walked back towards 'dog shit bridge' with a skip in my step, I feel invincible. I thank my creator for my good luck and good fortune in finding Genevieve. I have a quick chat with the voices on the way home and they all tell me not to fuck this up. I go home and go straight to bed. It's hot and sticky but I get to sleep pretty quick after necking a cold can to keep the sleep demons happy. I toss and turn most of the night but I get the sleep I require.

Chapter 24

After the usual morning routine and good morning text to Genevieve I leave my house at 7:24am. Genevieve never gets my texts in the morning as her phone is switched off as a precaution. It was already bright and sunny and looked like a great day ahead. "Oh fuck! Power Hour today, can't be fucked with that. Mind you, I could win some time off and finish early so maximum effort shitbag!" I walked the river path as I weighed up the positives and negatives of a power hour today. The negatives far outweigh the positives and I laugh to myself. For almost seven years in the same fucking job, having the same fucking conversations with the same fucking customers. I held on to the thought of winning an early finish.

As I walked the bend in the river path the sun shone brightly through the thick green council fences and straight into my eyes, temporarily blinding me. I carried on walking with my head ducked and looking down to the floor at the train track like shadows that tattoo the path I am on. As the impending trees block out the blinding sun my heart sinks into my belly. The horizon and everything in between hovers and vibrates, nothing stays still, the travellers have gone. I pull out my phone and call Genevieve, but no answer. I call her 30 fucking times and text her too but nothing goes through. I walk to the spot where less than 10 hours ago there were at least 20 vehicles and 30-40 people living there. They were gone. Not a trace.

I run back to our riverside spot hoping for some sort of message or sign from Genevieve to tell me what's happened, but all I see is the imprint of our bodies from the night before. I see the imprint where only a few hours ago we made love for the final time and I break down in tears. I lie on the flattened grass, it's still warm and I can smell Genevieve's perfume. I can still feel her presence, she's still there so I talk out loud to her. I ask her where she's gone? Why did this happen? Did her mother find out we were going to run away? Did her future husband find out about our affair? Where are you Genevieve? Don't leave me babe, I can't cope without you, I don't want to face life without you. Babe, why did you leave me?

I couldn't move from the riverbank and I cried for the first time in years as I felt a pain I'd never experienced before. I kept speaking to myself but I knew it was all fucked. We should have gone babe, why the fuck did we wait? Why did I stand there and send my beautiful Genevieve back to her mum? I'd fucked it up again. The best thing I'd ever had in my life and I fucked it up again. I spent the next two hours sat at the riverbank trying to process the situation. I was contemplating my life and what my next step was. I tried and failed to make sense of the situation as my devastation grew. I had to think rationally. Travellers move on, that's what travellers do. I had seen this scenario since I was a kid but I'd never had someone who belonged to that community taken away from me. The speed that this had all happened made me feel dizzy and nauseous. Genevieve wouldn't have gone without letting me know, she loved me too much. She wouldn't have not said goodbye. We had made too many plans, we were soulmates. I continued to cry. After the tears had run out, I ruled out suicide. I decided to drink myself to sweet oblivion every chance I could. I would let the pendulum swing decide my future from now on, I couldn't be fucked. I didn't want any say about my life anymore, I handed that off to someone else. From now on Captain Morgan and his good friend Wild Turkey would make my decisions for me.

My life had been changed so dramatically in a short period of time. All our plans and aspirations were thrown to the wolves and I had nothing to focus on. I would put more time and effort into my drinking. The beer would be chased by the bourbon or rum from now on. No short measures, no fucking amateur hour here cunt head, full commitment to the cause. My drinking was never the same again once the top shelf became an essential accompaniment to the beer and cider in the house. It consumed me and dragged me to the bottom of the bottle where it drowned me. It was an unescapable hell, an invisible prison of self-destruction. I stood up from our spot and brushed myself down after a couple of hours. I leave a personal memento at the riverbank that only we would understand and I walk back towards 'dog shit bridge.' I phone in sick for the rest of the week and I don't see or speak to another human being apart from the off licence owner who's till I will fill each night in return for loads of fucking drink.

Genevieve is gone, she's gone forever and I need to accept this. I need to feel thankful that I got to spend a few months with the most special human being I will ever meet. Even though I did finally accept it, it didn't stop me from texting Genevieve on her birthday every year. I never got a reply.

"Thank you for your time Genevieve, I wish you well. I hope the one child you will eventually have is slim and muscular like you'd always hoped our child would have been, with dark hair and a wild spirit. My sweet Genevieve, I will always love you. Goodbye."

I spend the next six months drunk. Is there a rock bottom? And is this drugs and alcohol, loads of fucking bad company and worse women, but no answers. Lots of blackouts and bruises but no reflection. Bucket loads of cocaine and self-pity but no redemption. A journey to hell, but still not my true self.

6 Months

Chapter 25

After developing gills from living at the bottom of a bottle for 6 months, I decided to give the real world a second chance. I agreed, against my better judgement, to attend that year's Christmas party in town. I was bored of the wino's, the slags, the barstool racists, the bigots. They were polluting my mind about how hard done to we were and if the world just listened to wino's we'd all be better off. Shut the fuck up! They were energy vampires who were sucking out any bit of positivity I had left towards life. I needed a change. Genevieve was gone and not coming back, I knew that now, no matter how I wished it wasn't true. This year's Christmas party was like last years, and no doubts like next years too. However, I would not know about next years as this would be by final one. I would continue to work for the bank for a number of years but as far as the social aspect of work, I fucked that off. I barely liked anyone in work anyway and it was so hard finding a good bunch of drinking buddies in a nest full of cunts.

I decided to get an early start so I bullied Pacman into meeting up three hours early. We trawled the back street Swansea pubs in the Sandfields area of the city. I was sick of the fucking trendy town bars we'd be in in a few hours. I wanted a shit hole with a pool table and a jukebox. We had a great early evening swig as we watched the daylight disappear to pitch black darkness in the matter of minutes. By this point both Pacman and myself were pretty well oiled up and doing speed wobbles up the street acting like kids. Slurring our words and arguing over the cigarette we agreed to go 50/50 on, we wrestled our way playfully passed the bouncers and into the Wind Street bar. It was about 8pm. Everyone else in the place, and I mean everyone, was stone cold sober.

Pacman and myself made clowns of ourselves but helped cut the tension of the stuffy atmosphere. Once the boring cunts got a few drinks in them it was leaving a decent night in the making. It was still early though.

"Why the fuck we here Pacman?" The question spilled out of my mouth as one by one the room started to swell with dickheads.
"Ten you know why. We've been told to turn up or the managers are going to use it as an excuse again to give us a shit end of year rating and therefore a shit bonus."
Pacman was right. Two years ago he missed the Christmas party and Jerome fucked him over in his end of year write up the week after, 'not promoting his brand and underperforming in social behaviours.'
Even though Pacman was good at his job and smashed all his targets, his refusal to kiss ass gave management the green light to shit on him. Missing the party two years ago cost Pacman about £3000. Money, he had earned. Money, he had worked hard for was taken away from him due to the opinion of a manager. No fucking statistics to back up the managers' decision, we were told it was done at the managers' discretion. The union had become toothless and it was common to see big titted, blonde haired union reps who were only doing it for time off the phone, laughing and joking at Jerome's desk when they should have been ripping his face off. £15 a month for my union subs and this slag's making plans to meet the boss for a drink on the weekend? Fuck off. Jerome's opinion that Pacman underperformed in his behaviours and didn't 'promote his brand' dragged his annual bonus from £3979 down to £839. Then on top of that, if you don't hit your behaviour requirements you are not eligible for a pay rise for another 12 months.

During these work parties the managers would hang around and try to be one of the gang and join in the banter. Drinking, swearing, sniffing, dirty jokes, anything that helped them be accepted for the evening. We'd learned quickly over the years that you didn't need to actually be in work to drop yourself in the shit. Every year, without fail, someone would attend the Christmas party and never go back to work again. Ever. Either ashamed of their behaviour, or most of the time having a phone call from HR to tell them their 'employment has been terminated for bringing the company into disrepute.' The bank's policy was, if it's an official work party, you are actually in your workplace and expected to adhere to those standards. That's pretty hard when you're in town drinking and snorting like a maniac, while trying to get your dick wet with any willing partner that owns a pussy. The drinks, and regular trips to the bathroom cubicles for a line had loosened everyone up. By 11pm you can actually witness marriages getting pissed down the drain for the sake of a drunken fuck. It will end up being the worst and most expensive fuck ever for most participants, a fuck that ends up as enjoyable as having a wank wearing a sandpaper glove. The lies and deception stories fill the room as wrong dicks will be entering wrong pussies. It's ok though, it's Christmas. These things happen at a Christmas party. Fuck Christmas.

Karley was there. She was married now and moved departments so I didn't see her much anymore, but we still fucked, maybe once or twice a year. Karley didn't bring her husband, instead she brought a 'friend' from Cardiff who she was in college with.

Natasha was very petite and elfish looking. She was very attractive and had a cracking little ass but she looked like she needed a good feeding before she got a good fucking. How wrong I was! I could see that Karley and Natasha were more than friends. Nothing was hidden and Karley said her husband was well aware that Natasha was her date for the night. It must have been a compromise the husband agreed to, and probably the only way he could stop his sex addict wife going out on a cock hunt every weekend.
"Ten this is Natasha. She doesn't work with us but we've known each other since college.''

I extended my hand to shake Natasha's. Her dark skin looked amazing wrapped around my pale, tattooed hand.

"Hey Natasha, nice to meet you." I gave the usual greeting that we all say but hardly ever mean. Still holding my hand tight Natasha signals me to lower my head, while at the same time discreetly gliding her hand over my bum, thigh and crotch.

"You're the famous Ten? Play your cards right and we'll let you fuck us both tonight. Karley's told me all about you loverboy."
I wasn't really looking for sex but I wasn't going to turn down the opportunity to fuck Karley again, who was a 9 in the sack. She'd playfully started this game by giving me a score of 8.5 Natasha would go on to get a 10 rating from both of us. She was a dynamite fuck and the most incredible lover either Karley or myself had ever had. Male or female, didn't matter, Natasha would fucking ruin you. Some people chose to bring their partners but most used common sense and didn't. Most, made the right choice.

Morgan was a quiet guy. A decent family man whom I had absolutely nothing in common with apart from the fact we worked in the same building. When we ever did speak it was always polite and good natured but due to the lack of common ground it turned awkward after about 90 seconds, but all in all Morgan was a good man. He didn't drink or do drugs. He turned up for exactly the same reason Pacman and myself had, the bonus money. Morgan had brought his wife Charlene and they had left their three children with Morgan's mother for the night. They made an odd couple. Even though Morgan was far from ugly he certainly wasn't pretty either. He was medium height, medium weight, medium build. He was your average guy with a hint of nerd and mastermind about him.

Charlene however was very attractive and seemed to know more people in the party than Morgan did. Pacman and Sadie were getting it on in a dark corner. It was the most odds on fuck of the night and it now looked certain to happen. Go on Pacman boy!!! I was necking shots with Karley and Natasha and having a good time. I'd found out that Natasha was actually married as well but separated from her husband. Karley pulls out a bag of pure and all three of us make our way to a private cubicle party. I end up in the female toilets with Karley and Natasha but there are other people in there as well as we can hear the snorting, grunting and fucking from some of the other cubicles. However apart from a little kissing and groping we're interested in the sniff not the sex. We wanted the good sex, not a fuck in a nightclub toilet. Hearing some commotion outside the door and familiar voices we all went silent and listened.

"What the fuck is going on? That's my wife!"
Morgan had gone looking for his wife and was told she'd gone to the bathrooms. Charlene had been necking free drinks all night and was pretty shit faced. She started to lose all her inhibitions as the alcohol kicked in and she started flashing her tits and arse at anyone looking. Charlene was on the dancefloor pretending to suck people off on her knees, male and female. She was a fucking mess. Morgan, now embarrassed by his wife's behaviour, retired to the bar for a stiff diet lemonade. "Hey Morg, gimme two minutes mate while I finish your wife off. I'll sort you out with a good rating pal don't worry, you'll get a cracking bonus. Now fuck off so I can come up your wife's arse."
It was Jerome. The dirty, sneaky, double crossing, fucking cunt.
As the door of the toilets opened and Morgan departed, Charlene, still with a dick in her ass, shouts for Morgan to get her another drink. Then begs Jerome to fuck her hard, like Morgan couldn't.

It turns out Jerome couldn't produce a good fuck either as a disappointed Charlene vacates the toilets giving Jerome shit about his little dick and inability to keep it up. Jerome didn't give a fuck, he walked out laughing. Morgan had walked out of the toilets and didn't say a word to anyone. He walked out of the bar and walked out of work, he never returned. From what his wife had told the rest of the moral-less slags she knew in work, Morgan had left her and also taken the kids. This was far from her first time getting caught with the wrong cock in her and Morgan had finally had enough. He packed up his three daughters who were all daddy's girls and fucked off to England. He settled in Glastonbury with his daughters and I never heard from, or spoke to him again. Charlene stayed friends with the people in work and ended up fucking half the call centre. I didn't really get what her agenda was. It's not like she was fucking professional footballers for a status fuck. Charlene was a sad, sad woman and didn't give a fuck she wouldn't see her daughters. As long as the parties and the fresh cock kept coming through on the conveyer belt of debauchery, she was happy. I knew Morgan a little but not enough to knock the boss out for him and lose my job, even though I really wanted to. Pacman and Sadie had already left. Or more accurately Pacman had been led by his shit secret Santa neck tie through the packed dancefloor, passed the bouncers and straight into a waiting taxi. Sadie wanted a fuck, and she would not be denied.

I left the Christmas party as a hypocrite as I got in a taxi with two married women, fully intending on fucking them both. Karley had been married about three years since the first time we slept together. We ended up in bed together a couple of times a year since. Karley had moved teams now so it was rare I even saw her in work. The three of us used each other's bodies to fuck away each other's sins. The sex was out of this world. Even though Karley and Natasha had been fucking each other for a decade, Karley was still blown away with Natasha's passion for us both that night. It was something to behold and I was a willing voyeur and an even more willing participant when the two sex kittens signaled me to get involved. We drank, we sniffed, we fucked and we all quickly agreed to a three way, no strings attached affair. This was no soulmate stuff. This was three sex addicts, involved in an ongoing, three way party fuck.

I needed a distraction in my life. I dived into the situation, tongue first!

Chapter 26

The first day back in work after the Christmas party is always interesting. People have had the whole of the weekend to process stuff and stew over it in many cases. The Monday walk of shame, thank fuck, didn't include me this time. The shamers sit with their heads in their hands, as they listen in horror to the stories of the Jekyll and Hyde character they became. A little alcohol and in some cases a little cocaine gave respectable people something to think about, in terms of their lives and how other people decided to live theirs. Other people, they remembered exactly what they did, and still didn't give a fuck. "If Morgan was fucking her right, I wouldn't have needed to give her a good bumming." Jerome was in his element as king rat. Like a fat peacock strutting around the office, laughing and shaking hands with his other dickhead mates about having sex with the drunk wife of one of his staff. "I don't know what his problem is, I bummed her. It's not like she can get up the duff." A person with no remorse for their actions, doesn't deserve the title of a person. They're a fucking slag. He was more pissed off that Morgan had not turned up for work leaving him a good man down on the phones. I hated the fucking guy. I couldn't think of words bad enough to satisfy the murderous things I was thinking in my head. What a cunt I thought. My thoughts went into overdrive trying to get some anger and frustration out.

"The fucking dictatorial, dearnful, discerptible, disorderly, draconic, diabolically, decaying, dishonest, disposable, domineering, daltonian, dastardly, diseased, cunt of a man." I felt a little catharsis. As more stories did the rounds, through the chatterboxes on the office floor to the shit stirrers the smoking den, in walks Pacman. With a fucking black eye! Now here was a story I wanted to hear!

"What the fuck happened to you? You didn't have a ruck at the party so where did you get that beauty? Deep colour in that fella, I like it. You'll have that for fucking weeks bro."
I could hardly contain my laughter as I continued to question Pacman, who was in no mood to talk.
"Fuck off you lot, leave me alone. I fell in the shower when I was hungover. It hurts like fuck."
The laughter stops and Sharkhead asks with a much concern as you'll get from the Shark
"Fucking hell mate, you ok? How's your head? Dizzy spells or blurred vision Pacman?"
"I'm ok Shark. I just want to sit down and get this fucking shift done so I can go home."
"You'll live son, hell of a shiner too, looks good."
In walks Sadie with a massive grin on her face.
"Oh, you like that do you? I gave him that!"
Sharkhead's big fucking shark mouth almost hits the floor. He looks like a Great White Shark with a broom rammed up its arse and eyes popping out,
"WAIT. What??? What the fuck? Hey Pacman, hey cunty lips, get fucking over here you lying cunt. What's this all about?"
Pacman's story wasn't convincing and we'd get the truth out of him eventually.
It was in the shower, and I did fall."
I was having none of it.

"No fucking way. Look at Sadie's smirk. Grab him Shark. Glug grab the fucker. Let's go for a smoke."

As we dragged Pacman outside for an old school interrogation, which would include lots of cigarettes being smoked and loads of threatening finger jabs to Pacman's chest, Sadie stopped us.

"Right you lot. Get the full story out of him. Have your laughs and wind ups, and then when you all get back in here, shut the fuck up!!!"
Like four naughty school kids being told off by the headmistress, we all stood and silently nodded our heads while pushing Pacman out of the door. We get outside and the smoking shelter's packed. I turn it into a military operation and start handing out jobs and directing people around.

"Over here lads. Away from everyone listening. Come on. Yeah I know it's fucking cold Pacman but I'm pretty sure you don't want them fuckers overhearing you. Glug roll some cigs. Pacman. Look at me. Listen now. Shut the fuck up, listen now. Right. From now on you only speak to Shark, got it? Sharkey you know how to question this little cunt, we got 15 minutes. On you go Shark." Sharkhead was good at this. He would ask simple questions, push the buttons, then watch the reactions. He was a card player, a good one too. If you're full of shit, Sharkey would read you like a fucking comic book in two minutes flat.

"Ok Pacman. We all know you went home with Sadie so we'll skip that shit for the time being, the sex stories can wait. Where did you get the black eye? And don't bullshit me son, you know I'll know." The Shark was sniffing, prodding, intimidating, but he needn't have wasted his effort. Pacman spilled the beans on the first spin. He told a story, that was so Pacman, it had Pacman stamped all over it, the fucking idiot. "Well boys. We got back to her house and we were all over each other straight away. My dick was hard as a rock, blah, blah,blah."On and on

Pacman droned about boring shit, until I clicked my fingers at the shark to keep on grilling him. Shark put a little aggression in his voice.

"The black eye shithead! Tell us about the fucking black eye."
"Ok, ok, gimme a minute, let me think."
"NO FUCKING THINKING, liars think. Talk you slag!"
In the meantime, Glug and me are pissing ourselves laughing at this double act. Pacman, shaking like a shitting dog, takes a deep breath and reveals it all. "We get back to her place and we're drinking, snorting, fucking, porn, the fucking lot. Great night. Anyway, we're watching porn and we're still both off our tits when Sadie demands I piss on her in the bath. I've never done this before, so I don't know what the etiquette is. I thought fuck it and just pissed all over her, head to toe. She fucking loves it."

"She gave you a black eye because you pissed on her?"
"No Glug. I'm coming to that. Can I carry on with my story?"
"Go on son, go on Pac, sorry man."
"So I go to bed and Sadie showers off and comes to bed as well. We both go to sleep. When I wake up in the morning Sadie's back in the shower. I've got a hardon and horny as fuck so decide to try my luck for a morning rub before she kicks me out for a taxi ride home. I strut down the hallway and can see the shower directly in front of me. I can see Sadie's naked, athletic body through the shower curtain and I remember our mad sex session that only ended an hour or two ago. I yank back the curtain with my left hand as Sadie turns and screams. She looks down to see a semi hard dick in my right hand. I look her directly in the eyes, and with a massive smirk on my face, unload a bladder full of dirty, stinking, nuclear orange piss, all over her beautiful clean body. Sadie took her right fist and rammed it into my left fucking eye. She then ordered me back to bed while she finished her shower."

By this point Glug and me are using each other for body support as we curl up in hysterics. Pacman went on to tell us that Sadie jumped straight back into bed after her shower, and gave Pacman the fuck of his life. Stood there with a cracking black eye and a big, dumb fucking grin on his face he announces.

"I'm in love boys!!!"

It turns out the feeling was mutual as Pacman and Sadie became an item. It was a good match between two great people.

Another good person in the office was Terry, and Terry didn't give a fuck about the walk of shame either. He lived his life as he wanted, and the only person Terry ever hurt was himself. Terry was a drinker. A heavy fucking drinker too. He carried himself with a happy demeanor and projected positivity to all around. I could see through it though. He wasn't happy. Terry camouflaged his sadness through jokes and a quick wit, along with discreet hand gestures that he only used when he was upset but trying to hide it. I guess he was hoping the slight of hand may distract from the language of despair. I was born on a barstool with a pint and a chaser in my hand, I could tell when some poor fucker was crying out for help. Terry was the kind of guy to suck your cock for a shot of sambucca at 2am, but ask him for his last Rolo and he'd tell you to fuck, right, off. He was a funny guy, proper good looking fucker too but a damaged soul. Terry treated himself like I had treated many women over the years, with no respect. I took a lot from Terry. Looking at someone I was the polar opposite of in terms of sexuality, I saw someone I actually identified with more than most people in my life. That wasn't good for Terry. I needed to help.

I gave Terry some great advice and it was advice I should be taking myself, but I never did. I told him drinking careers had short life spans and he would piss his 20s up against the wall and be in his 30s like me before he knew it. The thrill of the hit of the booze was gone, but Terry and I still chased it. We chased it like the holy grail of drinks. We searched for that one time in our childhoods, just one more time, the feelings we got when we would get drunk as kids. People like Terry and myself could never get passed the fact that we were chasing an invisible feeling. It was not a physical feeling, it was a mental one. It reminded us of the last time we were truly happy in life, before we crossed the divide, before we became experienced drinkers. We drank our childhoods down the drain for different reasons. Terry was scared to come out, so he drank. I was scared of happiness, I didn't feel it was for me.

My childhood was good and I was raised well, but I had a dark side that needed exploring, so I drank young. Alcohol was the thing we found to give us joy, many of us felt it was truly the only place we ever really belonged, even as kids. I'd been chasing an impossible feeling for 20 years, and the longer I chased it, the further away it got. But I still chased, I wasn't a quitter! I saw Terry as a young man with so much potential in his personal and professional life getting wasted. I hoped some of my words had a positive effect on him, but it's hard for people to take me seriously about drinking, when I'm stinking of the shit 24/7 myself. Terry was selling himself short and I'm not talking about sucking some fucker off for a drink. He should never have been in that position in the first place but he had no support network apart from his old Gran. I felt sad for him. I identified with Terry and I saw the sadness. I saw a sadness reflected in me. Gay, straight, male, female, rich, poor, black, white, whatever. Alcohol is the great redeemer. It's the one thing on earth that doesn't discriminate, it never has. It will fuck us all, regardless of circumstance.

Terry was not meant to be on this path. He was born gay, not damaged.

Me? I was born lost.

Chapter 27

After the 2008 financial crash they stopped us putting the 'hard sell' on the customers. The little adrenaline rush you got after working your ass off for a sale, had gone. The job became procedural and even more boring, they'd removed our cunning tricks from the role. The booze tables had been emptied and replaced with 'good behaviour' boxes, where you could anonymously nominate someone to be recognized for their good behaviours. The time off and early finishes dried up, as did all the other good rewards we got for mis-selling. We were robots now. Don't get me wrong, the mis-selling had to stop. Some of that shit was getting out of hand, we all agreed on that. What we did on a daily basis was immoral. We were rewarded greatly for these deeds and also, sometimes, bullied and intimidating into selling by managers over your shoulder. Literally stood over your shoulder, THREATENING you to sell! I shit you not. It wasn't a job for everyone. Fuck, it wasn't even a job for me, but I was good at it. I was a terrible chef but I was a great bullshit artist. With the gift of gab I was born with, the £10,000 extra I could pull down in bonuses over 12 months was taken away from me.

The selling and competition was furious as we all knew real money was at stake. Things did get shady and there would often be hushed whispers at the drinks machine or photocopier about a loop hole that could be exploited for our own personal gain. When all this got taken away the job died. The 'edge' had gone and the 'super sellers' had to check their personalities in at the door. It wasn't required for this job anymore. The job had been flipped on its head almost overnight. The shit sellers quickly became great performers, but for no extra bonus, no incentive to put up with the shit. While cowboys like me were sat down and told the ride was over. Either toe the line and read our scripts, or fuck off. None of the long termers wanted to leave as there were redundancies just around the corner and big cash sums, tax free up to

£30,000 up for grabs. With some of these people already sitting on 20 years service and a nice pension bubbling in the pot, semi retirement was just around the corner. Jumping ship now would be madness for anyone with over a decade of service in the back pocket. By 2012 I'd have 6 years of service under my belt and potentially looking at a redundancy pay off around the £10,000.Tax free! I'd bite their arm off, right up to their fucking shoulder for redundancy. But it never came. 2010, 2011, 2012 came and went in a drunken blur and people I'd worked with for 6 years were gone in a day. Some tears were shed but most skipped out the door of the call centre with a juicy cheque in their hands. I was genuinely happy for anyone who got redundancy from the sinking ship we were on. Once the cuts were made it was left to the reps on the phones to pick up the pieces. The call queues got higher, the customers got angrier and we got paid less.

I'd worked an extra three years, on the dream of a redundancy that never came to be. I was devastated. Sharkhead was too. Sharky was a lot smarter than me, and most of the other 800 or so people that were now left working in the building. He was more ambitious than the rest of us and had moved around the centre in various jobs. He'd got qualifications as a mortgage broker and was fully capable of running a full financial planning review with potential lending of up to a million pounds, signed off by nobody but him. Shark was wasted here. He had been shit on, so many times by management, that he knew hard work had fuck all to do with getting ahead in this place. It was down to kissing ass, which Shark didn't do.

It was a typical Monday morning and I was typically hungover. We had a power hour at 11am and Sharky wasn't up for it. He'd been arguing with his beautiful girlfriend all weekend and said he was about done with it all. Sharkhead always had stunning girlfriends even though he was an ugly cunt. The Power Hours now consisted of zero selling. It was now all customer satisfaction based. How much ass can you kiss in an hour and how many good behaviours can you smugly pat yourself on the back for? That's how winners were determined. I couldn't be fucked, and put zero effort in to patting myself on the back which pissed the managers off greatly as they could see first hand what a great job I was doing on the phones.

"Wilde! You could have won that Power Hour hands down, I was listening to your calls. Why didn't you report your behaviours?"
Jerome was out of his desk and giving me shit for my severe case of not giving a fuck.
"Jerome, it's not in my nature to bring attention to myself in work. Fuck I've been here almost a decade and I'm still unknown. I like it."
"That's not good enough Wilde. Your attitude to this job stinks and you have purposely not reported your behaviours. I'm putting you on report."

I couldn't fucking believe it. I was getting put on report, for being good at my job.
"Are you fucking serious? You said you listened to some of my calls?"
"You haven't reported behaviours for three months Wilde, I listened to the full hour. I heard some of the most exceptional customer service calls taken by a rep in this centre this year."
"And you're putting me on fucking report?"
"Your job role states, that it is your responsibility, to report your behaviours, so you can be judged against your peers in the end of year reports done by management."
"I didn't know they were good behaviours, I was just doing my job. Fucking hell where does it stop? Reporting a behaviour every time a customer gives a compliment? It's fucking ridiculous."
"If you were doing your job as per your job description you wouldn't be on report. But you weren't, so you are. Manager's report Wilde. We'll review your performance in one month and decide if any disciplinary action needs to be taken."

"Crack on shipmate, see how many fucks I give."

I hadn't called anyone shipmate in over six years, as no cunt on civvy street was ever my shipmate. I was just being obnoxious now, and that meant Jerome was about to get a fucking slap if this carried on. And then, Sharkhead saved us both. He saved my job and a good chance he saved my freedom. He definitely saved Jerome, from getting a few left handers that would have made a right mess of his fat face. Alternatively, a few right handers that would have left his face like a horror show. Either way didn't matter to me as I had grenades for fists. I didn't have much brains and the 'big dick' train didn't stop in the hospital on the day I was born. But I was blessed with knock out power in each hand, I didn't even have to learn it.

Sharkhead was more aggressive than normal with his customers as our new team manager Jacqui listened in nervously. Jacqui was 20 and had been with the bank less than 12 months and was a manager already. She was also involved in the world's worst kept secret affair with Jerome. Everyone knew about it, including Starr, Jerome's long suffering wife. Starr had known Jacqui for years, since she was a child. She even babysat her on a few occasions.

He was now stood up, clearly frustrated with his customer while pointing at the screen and rubbing his head. Sharky tried dumbing it down as if he were talking to a 6-year-old but the customer still wasn't getting it. The Shark had taken the bait, and bit.
"You're a fucking window licker son. I bet when you come, your face looks normal."

The last call Sharkhead would ever take in the place, as he slams his headset into the screen and walks out. I'm sat in code 661 not taking any calls. Rearranging Jerome's face goes to the back of my mind as I get up and follow Sharky to the smoking den, where he's obviously going. I find Sharkhead stood on the lush green grass about 15 yards away from the smoking shelter. It's far enough to give us the required privacy from the gossips in the den.

"Mrs fucking with your head Sharky boy?" My tone is quiet and serious as I take the cigarette Sharky has pre-rolled and light it up.
"Ahh Ten, it's more than that mate. I've had enough son. Mrs, job, city living, all the pricks I have to deal with. They can all fuck off. I don't want it anymore, I'm done."

These types of rants and verbal handing in of notices regularly took place in the smoking area. At least three times a day you'd hear some disgruntled fucker say they're going to hand their notice in, but they never did. Sharkhead never talked like that though. Yeah he bitched and moaned like the rest of us but it was normally accompanied by a joke or hilarious put down. There was none of that as Sharkhead let me be the first to know he intended on handing his notice in. Once he finished a couple of cigarettes first.

"The jobs changed Ten. I can't do it anymore son, I don't fucking need it. I don't need this fucking life anymore, I'm sick of it."
Sharkhead spoke eloquently and passionately. I don't think he was trying convincing himself, I could see he was plenty convinced already. Sharkhead was preaching to me. He knew what a fuck up I was, and he knew he was not going to be there anymore, to warn me when the backstabbers and grasses were up to their normal two faced shit. We'd looked out for each other since day one when I started that job. Shark was already there. I trusted him 100%.

As he carried on talking the whole perspective changed, from the job, to the world, to life, to the universe. Shark was unloading his burdens and setting himself free right in front of my eyes. I could see a man changing his life as we spoke, it was inspiring. And I was inspired but I was also still gutless.

"The whole world on my fucking phone and I dislike people now more than ever. The politics man, I don't get it, I keep getting it wrong. I think I'm out of touch Ten, with society and with what we want as a society. The Tories have had five years and it looks like they'll get another five. I don't like the smell son, it smells rotten. But I'm a sore loser too." I think Sharky was going through a 50% breakdown and 50% rebirth as he let everything out to me and held nothing back.

"I've been thinking of moving overseas Ten, fresh start, you know? But why the fuck should I? I could move to the fucking moon and still get annoyed with people on social media and all the other shit. I want to start love living in Wales, and stop hating living in the UK, it's not good for my head. I'm going to buy some land in the countryside, build a house. I'll write books and go walking everyday. The drink's done mate. I've been off it for weeks and it felt good, until life dragged my spiritually unprepared ass back on the drink last week. I feel like shit all the time with drink, I'm just gonna smoke weed from now on, fuck it!" As he went on I listened intently, and happily smoked the cigarettes he kept offering.

Shark was clever, he'd been stacking his deck for a few years in preparation for this moment. I knew he was a bit of a casino magnet as I'd been there plenty of times with him, pissed to the eyeballs playing roulette. What I didn't know, until now, was that Shark had amassed over £420,000 profit from online poker. NOBODY knew this, apart from me. It showed a great deal of trust and respect, and Shark knew his secret was safe with me, he'd kept plenty of mine over the years.
"If they don't sack me Ten, I'll quit anyway. Today's the day. I've put 12 years into this place, the best years of my life for these fuckers. My pension looks good and I can confidently say I'm 34 and have zero job

satisfaction. I've got a tidy wedge of cash hidden from every fucker and a little invested in some cryptocurrency shit, supposedly it'll be worth a good return in a few years, who knows."

Sharkhead put out his third cigarette and thanked me for the chat, even though I hardly said 5 words.
"Right, off to see these fucking idiots Ten. I'm going now, fuck the notice, I'm never going back on the phones in here. Give me half hour son and I'll come see you before I fuck off, we'll arrange a leaving drink with some of the old crew. I'll give myself a weekend drinking pass. It'll only last a night as I'll be fucked the next day. Anyway, catch you in a minute son."

Shark came to say goodbye to the team and it was quite emotional. Jess and Sadie were devastated but happy, when they found out he quit and was not sacked. He didn't tell anyone else about his money or his plans and he left before lunch. "Off for a spliff," were the last words spoken by Sharkhead in the building. I still saw him now and again until he moved six months later. By the age of 36 he'd fucked off the writing and become a 'YouTuber.' His natural skill for all things poker and gambling mixed with one of the best sense of humors on the market, he was a hit.

When I last spoke to the Shark he was living in the Welsh countryside, with shit telephone reception. He had a decent online set up so was always available online if I needed a chat. He eventually sorted the phone signal. He told me he'd bought a cottage and was loving life. He said he was sat on about £2 million. That really meant Shark was now sat on about £4 million. Like I said, clever guy. When I first met him, he told me to watch my back in this place, and to always keep my cards close to my chest in whatever I do. He'd kept the cards close to his chest, in work, in the casinos, on the websites, and in life. Sharkhead was winning, once he opened his mind and walked out of the cell inside it. He went on to different life, he found his serenity. I still didn't know what that word even meant.

Chapter 28

The turnover in the centre was high and people were leaving with regularity. I did miss having Sharkhead around but after a week or two the sad reality is, you're forgotten about. We like to think we leave unfillable shoes and the place will fall apart when we go. It never happens. By lunchtime tomorrow our seat will be filled by another fat arse and our name will rarely be spoken again. Like a fart in the wind, we quickly disappear without a trace.

The job kept me paid and was a doddle but mixed with all the heartbreaks and alcohol, my spiritual bank remained empty. Any holiday time I took was spent in the Swansea bars, with an occasional gig thrown in here and there, which was the only time I really travelled anymore. Foreign holidays were few and far between. If I could have stuck my dick in a bottle of Wild Turkey I would have never needed to go out. Sex was a drug for me. I wanted the hit but not the come down. My love life had consisted of a ridiculous amount of one night stands with a relationship popping up here and there, but nothing ever more than a few months. Living alone as an alcoholic who talked to voices could sometimes get frustrating, I got on my own nerves most of the time. The voices became a welcome distraction.

Since the Christmas party I'd been involved in a three way affair with Karley and Natasha. We'd picked up where we left off and partied together about once a month. In the meantime, Natasha had started showing up at my place on her own about once or twice a week. We began our own private affair which we kept from Karley but she eventually figured out by the way we acted around each other. When the three way affair was done until the next time, Karley had her husband. Natasha and me only had each other. Karley was only a tourist to the misery, Natasha and I were full born nationals. Mine was drink, Natasha's was whatever was on offer. Karley and Tasha still had their own private affair too, which was a decade old, but according to Tasha it was dwindling out. Karley was now spending more time with her husband on weekends while Tasha embraced the hedonistic lifestyle. Which involved regular trips to me. Our sex life intensified even more with just the two of us involved. As lovers we were a perfect match but as a serious couple it would be a trip to hell. We would drag each other to rock bottom quicker as a duo and we both knew that.

The connection I had with Karley, even before Natasha was on the scene, was all about lust. She turned me on and I wanted to fuck her, that's basically it. I had that lust and those intentions for Tasha too, probably even more, but we also had a deeper connection, a common ground. We were both addicts. When we looked at each other we both saw a broken soul looking back. Our spirits crushed a little bit every time we realised our presence in each other's lives would not end well. If we ever decided to get sober and clean, we would never get better together. Instead, we would take each other to places both physically and mentally that we may never return from. I couldn't help Natasha and she couldn't help me, but we could fuck each good. We fucked each other senseless and partied and talked. We kept each other company because we didn't really like anyone else.

Tasha's father was Somalian and her mother was from somewhere in the Rhondda valleys. They met in Cardiff, while in college in the 1980s and made a new life for themselves in the city. Tasha's skin was dark, and so smooth. She took pride in her appearance and personal hygiene but her insides must have been fucking rotten, as she hardly ate and partied all the time. Her father became a successful barrister and earned a good living. He quickly moved his young wife and baby daughter out of the rough inner-city areas. Life was perfect for young Natasha and she loved her father more than anything in the world. Tasha's dad was killed in car accident when she was 14 years old. It turned her world upside down. Her mother? Tasha never really felt a connection to her mother and the feeling was mutual. Tasha's mother enjoyed the high life as her husband went up the pay scale quickly due to working his ass off. In Tasha's own words about her mother. "She means nothing to me Ten. She never wanted me as a kid. When dad was around, and even when he died she still didn't want me. I couldn't give a fuck anymore, I haven't seen her for years and don't intend to either."

Tasha ended up moving in with her Auntie Jo and her boyfriend Uncle Mus, a few weeks after her dad's funeral. They both loved Tasha like she was their own child and Tash told me she loved them both dearly in return. "Auntie Jo and Uncle Mus showed me more love in a couple of years than my mother ever showed me in her whole life. I would trade my mother's life to save either one of those people in the blink of an eye. I wouldn't even think about it."

When Tasha was 17 she was attacked by a pack of cunts who decided they would rape her as well. Tasha told me the full story and I had to hold back my tears, in order to hold on to my anger. I was shaking. I was furious. Why couldn't have I been there to stop it? Why didn't someone help? What the fuck is up with these fucking guys? The fucking shit eaters, I wished them dead. Uncle Mus wasn't there either.

Uncle Mus was a former Tongan rugby player who moved to Treorchy in the 1990s when rugby union officially became a professional sport. He gained a cult following in the Rhondda for being one of the league's top scorers, while playing for one of the league's worst teams. He could have gone to bigger teams for better money, but he'd found his place in the world. He loved it. Unsurprisingly it turns out Uncle Mus was as hard as coffin nails. After his rugby career ended, he quickly and easily stepped into his doorman shoes and made a living as a well respected bouncer in Cardiff.

Within a few hours of the rape Uncle Mus had used his connections to find out who was responsible. The police had been informed of the attack already, and were told the full names of all three men involved. According to Uncle Mus' source, they were due to be arrested the next morning. Uncle Mus went to the hospital to make sure Tasha was ok and then he took her home with Auntie Jo. On the way out of the hospital Tasha remembers Uncle Mus telling one of the male porters he knew at the hospital to 'clear a few fucking beds.' He then proceeded to visit each address of the three attackers, kick their front doors down and release a blast of Tongan fury that would invade these cunts dreams for life. Tasha told me two of the rapists were lucky to be alive. One of the sick fuckers never left the mental hospital. He thought Uncle Mus would find him and finish the job. Why did he think this? Because Uncle Mus had told him in court, and he told the judge at the same time.

When he plead guilty to all his charges the judge passed sentence. I don't think Uncle Mus did himself any favours when he corrected the judge on the attempted murder charge.

"Your Honour. The only thing I was attempting, was to NOT murder the little cunts. I regret nothing."
7 years.

The three rapists were sentenced to 3 years, 18 months and 18 months. Natasha was devastated with the loss of her uncle and her downward spiral started from there. Her Auntie Jo did everything she could but

Tasha was well into adulthood by the time Uncle Mus was released from prison four years later. Tasha was a different person by now. Through repetition she had learned life was a series of disappointments and good men were taken from her too early. She was such a beautiful woman it masked the pain she hid inside. But I could see it, I could always see it. Apart from fucking, drinking and drugging, we often enjoyed sitting on the kitchen floor in a drunken stoned daze watching the washing machine spin. We'd sometimes sit in a comfortable silence as we both watched the same thing but took a different experience from what we saw. We'd drift in and out of conversation while drinking and smoking sat on the kitchen floor for hours. I think it was therapeutic for us both. Grimey souls taking pleasure in watching things get clean. I didn't realise the significance of these times until years later.

I'd sometimes go to Cardiff on day trips with Tasha to visit her friend. Another addict, another threesome but a different Tasha. I didn't like Tasha's friend and for the time she was in her company, I didn't like Tasha either. I still fucked them both though. The conversation bored me and even Natasha bored me on these days. The two of them would constantly disappear and come back in the room 10 minutes later looking a few IQs lighter each time. The downer of choice was heroin. I was sick of my own downer addiction, so I had no plans of upgrading from booze to smack, I'd be dead in a month. I don't think Natasha or myself really knew each other. We just knew the cartoon characters we'd both become in life. I was coming up to my mid 30s and I felt no guilt in having no commitments to Natasha, as I knew she didn't have the commitment to whatever our relationship was either. She would often say to me that she would prefer it if it was me all the time. Tasha wasn't a liar but I didn't believe her. I would laugh and brush it off with a joke and a drinks top up, all while changing the subject. We'd then fall into another drink and drug fueled fuck before falling asleep in each other's arms.

I sometimes hoped I wouldn't wake up and just carried on in a never ending dream, not having to come back and deal with the monotonies of life. Tomorrow always comes though, and I never know if I'm sad or just surprised that I'm still alive. One day, tomorrow won't come. It will happen to us all. We will all have our last February.

Chapter 29

I still hadn't come to a point in my life where I was comfortable in my own company, I could easily start a fight in an empty house.
I kept my mind active by watching movies and listening to music, all of course while drinking like a fucking degenerate.

Some days I didn't want to see anyone. I didn't want to speak to anyone. And I sure as shit didn't want to go out. Luckily on this cycle of male PMT it fell on a Saturday morning, on a full wolf moon. It was cold, dark and depressing, so I checked the supplies in my fridge. There were enough cans to get a bull lashed. Plus, a bottle of Morgan's Spiced, a bottle of Wild Turkey, half a bottle of Jack, a bottle of QC, two bottles of red wine, and half a litre of decent vodka left in the shed from a previous outside drinking sesh in the cold while burning rubbish. I had no need to go out for a couple of days. I took a long hot shower, had a shave and brushed my teeth. I put on clean clothes and done my hair in the mirror using one hand, while locking the front door with the other. The thought of all the alcohol in the locked house and the magnificent solo party I was about to have. Booze and Hip-Hop was the order of the day. The two things in my life that had always stayed consistent. I knew what both would bring me, they satisfied my craving. I needed them.

My music collection was vast and my music knowledge was decent for a pub quiz level. I'd grown up around music since I was born, taking a strong influence from my father. He'd immersed me in a childhood of blues, soul, and jazz, along with the black musicians who'd invented rock and roll which gave birth to modern music as we know it. I soaked it all up like a sponge, all genres, nothing was off limits. But Hip-Hop was different, it wasn't my oldman's, he didn't understand it, it was mine. I embraced it like an eager student and started with the Menace to Society soundtrack I bought on my 13th birthday. I'd rented the movie when it first came out because I liked the cover, and even though the film was great, I fucking loved the soundtrack even more. I worked my way back in history, grabbing hold of any bit of rap I could get my hands on. At the time it was as rare as rocking horse shit in the UK, let alone Wales!

I switched on the stereo and hit the shuffle button of my iTunes. My Saturday officially started with the snake hiss of my first ice cold can of lager being cracked open. The music comes through the well used speakers and fills the room with a familiar tune and appropriately named song, 'Doing Dumb Shit.' Considering I planned on drinking myself to blackout I couldn't think of a more perfectly titled opener. Ice Cube's lyrics ripped through the speakers. "When I was young I used to hang with the 7th graders, little bad motherfucker playing space invaders." What a start to the day! A classic. 4500 songs to drop and my shuffle button drops a classic. Cube made many great albums but Death Certificate tops the lot for me. As far as I was concerned, Ice Cube was sat at the top table of MCs.

I excitedly necked the can I was drinking in three greedy swigs as I stood in front of the stereo, head bobbing, as happy as a fat chick in a disco. I'm hyped up but need to calm down. Another four songs like that and I'll be smashed before 8:30am. Next track.
"I'm 22 with a motherfucking beer belly, some say I'm an OG already."
No luck with the hype dying down, as another favourite of mine is already inbound, along with another can, AND fucking Dev decides it's

time for the voices to start. Using my mouth for his thoughts he spits out his usual bile.

"Yeeeaaahhh, same as you fat boy! 22 with a motherfucking beer belly, 34 and it's even bigger now ya fat cunt!"

Cheers Dev, good morning to you too.

I look sideways at nobody, as there's nobody there. I look sideways anyway.

"Shut the fuck up Dev, you're ruining the Spice One track, I'm starting it again now. It's too early for you cunts, come back at lunch when I need you."

No response.

With the early adrenaline rush now running on fumes I decide to sit down and chill for the next few hours, no doubts a bit of kitchen dancing at lunchtime, half pissed. As I slouch into the dark leather sofa I've spent so many nights on, I feel like I'm in my safety cocoon. A few sticky spillages not cleaned up properly in the past, leave a stale beer smell in two areas but it's not bad. It's a good conditioned and well used bit of furniture, with a history that would make the fake casting couches of the porn channels blush. The shuffle is treating me like royalty as I'm blessed with Paparazzi, Keeping the faith, and Speedlaw, one after the next. The buzz I get when I hear the car revving its engine in the Speedlaw intro and then accelerating like a race car at the start line. The drums, the DJ scratching, the strings, the beat, that fucking beat man! Even before Mos goes off like Ayrton Senna in a Marlboro, leaving competitors in his wake, I'm fucking buzzing. And then Ref opens his fucking killjoy mouth, like Ned Flanders on a stag do.

SLOW DOWN YOU TWAT

"Fuck off Ref, I'm enjoying," was my immediate response.

I had to wait a few seconds for the Ref's response, and it shocked me. Ref swore and cursed a lot considering he was supposed to be a voice of reason. He actually swore more than the rest of us put together. His foul language was normally a red rag to the Dev bull, and there was nothing Dev liked better than an excuse to have a pop at Ref. But even Dev kept his shit stirring mouth shut on this one.

"COME ON TEN, COME ON BOY, JUST PACE YOURSELF. SLOW DOWN OK."

And that was it. No swearing, no shouting, no anger, no insults. Just concern. Considering Dev didn't pipe up to have his usual say on the matter I chalked this one up as a Ref win. I slowed the pace.

The music continued as I placed a bet on the afternoon's football matches. I never expected to win but it was an afternoon's entertainment for £10 so I wasn't bothered about losing it. However, it was nice when a winner would come in, it gave me something different to celebrate. I would celebrate a win as hard as I would celebrate a loss. With my bet placed and lunchtime tapping me on the shoulder, the beat to Halfway Thugs kicks in. This beat always inspires two things. More volume and more alcohol. Another can destroyed and another opened. Like a well trained marathon runner knows when lactic acid is going to affect their race and performance, an alky knows when the darkness is creeping in. Pick up the pace for a couple of cans and all will be good.

I go for a walk on dangerous ground with Keith Murray, where we talk of the dayz of way back and the killaz in the park. Getting High & Mighty on the meaning while the Arsonists rage a blaze to the eve of war. A Cool Breeze whispers in the wind to watch the hook, while the Beatnuts and Dead Prez tell me to take a look around. I look in the fridge and it still looked stocked as I grab a cold beer. KMD got me looking at the sweet premium wine on the kitchen counter top and Big Pun tells me to beware. I think about my hangovers with Gift of Gab and how they make you feel that way. I process the words and beats in my mind. While it's testament to Cormega I'm not living Biggie's everyday struggle, as the psalms hit like a rhino from book number 7 infecting my brain like a born killer, reminiscent of Scarface with a scared eyebrow in 1983 living the Miami life with Ras Kass on the final verse to take it home.

The music plays on as I zone in and out of mid-morning drunkenness while doing speed wobbles in the corridor as I stagger to take a piss.
"put some Big L on"
Dev piped up like a pisshead at the DJ booth.
"Big L Ten, I'm up for that" came the voice of my reason and wellbeing, Gel. "We all like L, good choice."
Very rarely did Dev and Gel agree on anything but even when they did, Dev still couldn't be nice.
"C'mon Ten, even the fun sponge over there agrees with us."
The speakers erupt with menace as the classic track Devil's Son takes me back to a happier time as I bust out L's verses word for word just like I did when I was 16 years old. That track is then followed by the 7 minute freestyle with Jay-Z, and then representing on a Showbiz beat to show the world L was a different mustard, even back then.

I flick the shuffle button back on as I break down Tupac's lyrics and hear new stuff, words I never heard before in songs I'd been playing for 20 years. "I was raised in the city, shitty ever since I was an itty bitty kiddy, drinkin liquor out my momma's titty. And smoking weed was an everyday thang in my household, and drinkin liquor til you out cold." It was crazy how the lyrics I'd been listening to for so long had started to get a deeper significance to me personally. The words shook me, spun me, digested me, and shit me out. Pac's words did that to me and in doing so made me feel totally inadequate as a writer, but none the less inspired to try. A good friend over the years and provider of support when I didn't have a support network I could trust during dark personal times.

Dre got me stranded on death row reading Common's book of life, while down in the rec room Scaramanga got me holding new cards. It's a conflict if I get a Royal Flush not to yell Geronimo and go all in, cos shit is real. A.Z. telling me he feels for you like I do when I watch the rise and fall of Elliot Brown, who was paid in full with 7 minutes of madness.

I'm pretty much tanked up now as I become a double fisted drinker with a Morgan's Spice and ginger beer mixed in one hand and half a can of lager attached to the other hand all day that keeps getting replaced every 20 to 30 minutes. I shovel the shit down my pleading gullet. I reminisce about the good times, after hours with the tribe, a perfect track to set up LL's rampage of EPMD's classic as I slur my way through all three verses. I'm a fucking addict to this shit, jack me up and pump my veins with it. The dense rhymes of soul on ice pave the way for Pudgee to act a phat bastard while checking out the avenue. It's treacherous as Brooklyn/Jersey get wild but the sunny meadowz make me feel like I own America 2. Walking with uncommon valor, I could hold my head up high in the ill street blues. Quik is the name but long is the struggle as it's been 93 til infinity since I was last a soul carrying vessel.

My soul of mischief explores the verbal intercourse through the lights, camera and action, glamour, glitters and gold. I unfold the scroll, plant seeds to stampede the globe, when I'm deceased and at peace, hearing the symphony of the grand finale. I keep telling myself to drink more, drown the misery, hide the pain, kill the demons. Ain't it good to you? No. And I don't know what it represents anymore. I've got inherited scars that I don't understand, it's dark, and hell is hot. I open the wild turkey as I finish off the rum. I drink, I forget, I remember, I drink. I'm Mobb Deep in a drunken fairground of a brain, addled and confused. A Prodigy told me the whole world's going insane, so I fill my brain up with Henny and drink away the pain. I think the whole world's lost its brain. I sip away on the liquor, and drink away the pain.

It's late, I'm drunk and crying, I'm slippin, I'm falling, I can't get up....Blackout

Chapter 30

Another lost weekend and another hungover Monday morning. I filled my desk with plastic cups of water that would give me a genuine reason to visit the toilet and have some time off the phones. On my third trip of the morning to the drinks machine I bumped into AG and we had an as always interesting conversation. I left my conversations with AG feeling like I could have spoken to him all day. He worked in a different department to me but I would bump into him now and again either by the drinks machine, photocopier or the smoking den. I'd chat to him maybe 2-3 times a month. AG was a nice guy, very quiet and unassuming. He dressed smartly and with his long ginger dreads down to his ass, he looked like a well dressed hippy. He was well spoken and knew his job inside out. I didn't see AG ever lose his rag but he would sometimes just stare at idiocrasy from behind his glasses, until the person got the hint that they'd just said something fucking stupid. Only then would AG continue speaking. The way he did it amused me greatly. Over our conversations we chatted candidly about the upcoming Isle of Man TT and the summer music festivals just around the corner. Both AG and myself were bikers but he'd actually been to the TT and gone round the track on his bike too. He was an easy going and interesting guy, caught up in a stressful goldfish bowl type of job. I used booze to kill the stress my job brought on me. However, I used booze to kill the majority of stresses life brought to the table as well. But this chapter is not about me, it's about AG, so let me carry on please.

AG seemed a bit of a straight head when it came to drugs and alcohol. If it wasn't for his three foot ginger dreads he'd go unnoticed in a building of 800 people. I'd never heard anyone say anything bad about AG but then again, I'd never heard anyone say anything good either. He wasn't talked about and his name was never banded around the office as a top performer. He came in, done his job and fucked off home. He blended in, kept his head down and to 99% of the people that worked in the centre, AG, simply was just not there. It was like sometimes he didn't even exist.

After a few weeks I stopped seeing AG. People moved on in this place with regularity and people you've seen every day for the last 10 years sometimes just go and are never seen again. This was not strange; it was just the job. People would go and sometimes come back. A girl I saw in the smoking shelter now and again told me that she left the bank over a year ago and has had two jobs since returning to the call centre. I didn't even know she'd left. It was a place that you may only see someone you know once a year, possibly less depending on shift patterns and you end up only ever bumping into someone by luck or coincidence. It wasn't an unusual occurrence here.

Walking in circles around the empty smoking shelter one afternoon, I was enjoying the peace. The usual noise and chatter, laughter and banter was gone. I wasn't getting bumped into by people trying to enter or leave the shelter all while holding hot coffee in their hands, fucking dickheads. The regular faces of the usual corners were not there to pollute me today. The snakes, the rats, the good, the bad, the ugly, the VERY fucking ugly, the predators, the prey, the liars, the thieves, the backstabbers, the snitches, the cunts…..Empty. There was nobody there and I felt alright, I was in a decent mood actually. I enjoyed these moments of peace and self reflection. I yearned for more of it in my life. Booze didn't provide me with that anymore, I don't think it ever did. I was being coparented by alcohol, chaos and depression. They were not a good mix.

Standing in a crowded small area you don't get to see the full picture. People and things get in the way of where your thoughts mean to take you. We become distracted by things that are not important and our lives pass us by. My spiritual potential was being held prisoner in the belly of the hulking building. The phone calls from piss ant customers blocking my ears with shit every day. My soul on the other hand, was drowning at the bottom of a bottle being held by my own hand. I haven't got anything or anyone to blame for that, apart from the dickhead holding the bottle.

I thought of AG and how I hadn't seen him for about for a while. I thought he must have just had enough and said, fuck it, I'm off. After a bit of time with my own thoughts I asked a few people when I went back in if they'd seen AG recently? Hardly anyone I asked even remembered him, let alone of where he went. Did he even exist? Or was he a figment of my imagination like the four voices of the apocalypse? Another drinking buddy to add to the already complicated list of personalities I could choose to be each day. If he was real or imagined the simple fact is the fucker never came to see me no more, so I just put it down to another interesting individual who'd passed through my life and moved on.

A year or so later I heard a rumour, a crazy rumour. AG was a bomb maker and a crystal meth chef! He set up a make shift lab in the kitchen of his dwellings.
"No fucking way Glug! You're full of shit son. All the bloods run from your head to that big dick of yours, you crazy fuck."
But Glug was having none of it, he was adamant.
"Look Ten, look. Come here Ten, look I found it you childish prick, look."

113

Glug handed me the phone as I read from the BBC News Website "A man who admitted possessing a range of explosive chemicals and weapons has been jailed for six years."
"Fucking hell Glug."

The report went on to say how AG had made a load of drugs at his house, including crystal meth. For personal use. He had stun guns dotted around the house disguised as torches, cans of pepper spray too. AG had been on the dark web, buying the ingredients for crystal meth. He'd been flagged up somehow and the police were informed. The cops found a copy of the anarchist's cookbook and a US Army Special Forces guide to unconventional warfare devices. This contained instructions, detailed instructions, to make bombs. Along with a kitchen full of all sort of chemicals to make all types of shit. There was no evidence to suggest that AG had planned to use the weapons or sell the drugs. The depending solicitor said the defendant had been addicted to drugs for 10 years. The prosecutor said that some of the weapons had been purchased after an argument between AG and his neighbours. The judge ruled that AG was obsessed with explosives rather than maliciously motivated. He described AG as more of a nerd than a threat.

AG admitted 23 counts of possessing an explosive substance, along with charges of possessing prohibited weapons and class A drugs. Judge Thomas said at sentencing that AG was "not connected with any terrorist organisations or groups or movements." A solo crazy cunt, in my words. I liked AG and was not about to stick the boot in. He was always gracious and polite to me and I enjoyed our conversations. He didn't hurt anyone, sell any drugs, or blow anything up. He just had a really weird fucking hobby. And highly fucking illegal as well.

I think AG was doing a bit of homemade schooling and getting crystal methed off his tits for free, if I'm honest. No further information is known as he was sent to prison. He was a nice guy but maybe not the best neighbour. An accidental explosion from his meth lab or a crazy bomb gone wrong could end up being flattening a few buildings. I can't imagine what the bond is going to be for AG on his first place back on civvy street, the landlord will skin him. "The Flat is yours AG, but as you're a convicted bomb maker your bond will be fucking £2 million, just incase your start getting flashbacks to your old Walter White days."

AG won't be long getting out or probably even out, depending on when you are reading this. With an easy going character and good work ethic, of which AG had both, I'd imagine he'd been looked at for early release with good behaviour. This is when it's important to note your good behaviours, not when you've helped a customer verbally wipe their own ass. Do they give early releases for bomb makers and meth chefs? Fuck knows. But if you're out, good luck and I hope you're doing alright. Get some new hobbies in prison, ones that don't involve getting you locked back up or blown the fuck up.

Chapter 31

Work was getting worse and it was becoming a struggle to drag myself to the place each day. The hangovers got worse the older I got and I could feel it taking its toll more than it did before. I don't know if I wanted to drink anymore but I know I also didn't really want to stop yet.

Terry had come into work devastated the week before with the news his beloved grandma had passed away. Terry had a difficult early life and had never really felt accepted anywhere he had been. Apart from with grandma. She accepted Terry from day one with whatever he was, just as long as he was looking after himself, which he wasn't. He'd lived with her from his early teens up until leaving for college at 18. I'd never seen a person look so broken and alone. He ended up going home as it was no good for him being in work so Sadie and Jess took him home when their shifts finished. I felt better that the poor fucker had someone to keep an eye on him with the state he was in. Sadie and Jess could fuck around with the best of us but they could also flip the switch and becoming caring and compassionate in a second. It was important in a place like this, to have these people. There were some great individuals who provided needing people with valuable support, and for the right reasons too and not a pat on the back.

After Terry went home Jerome spent all day going on about how the queues were busy and Terry had let the team down.
"His grandmother who brought him up from a kid has just fucking died. What do you expect? Him to take calls? A lot of good that would do anyone, including the customers."
I'd had enough of Jerome after all these years, I didn't even bother hiding my distain for the guy anymore. I tried not to give him the time of day if I'm truly honest, and walk the other way. He was lower than a snake's belly.
"I don't care if his fucking grandma's dead Wilde, she's not his immediate family therefore he should be in work. That's company policy.
"That may be the case Jerome but Terry's a union member. I'm sure a union rep would love this nice easy case. He could be off for months if he wanted so give him a break for a week or two. He's always been a good and reliable phone rep, never let anyone down, he's earned some compassionate leave."
"Compassionate leave? You're soft Wilde, to manage this place you have to stick to the company policy book, no fucking about. I thought you were in the army, tough guy and stuff."

I'd even stopped correcting ignorant fucks about my previous career. If they still didn't know after all these years they obviously didn't give a fuck. And I was ok with that. I had no intention of wasting my time on a pointless conversation that would end up coming up time and time again. "I took more from the military than trying to be a tough guy pal, something you'd never understand." Jerome walked off to another team to spout more of his shit. As long as he was out of my face I didn't care.

Terry came in two days later and worked the rest of the week in full. He was still in shock but was doing better and I begged him to go home, but he said he was good. He was in a lot of pain but I could see heading in the right direction.

When he came in on Monday he told me he had been sober all weekend. He hadn't even thought about drinking. Even though the sadness was still there I saw the chiseled sign on positivity on his face that wasn't there when he left on Friday. He'd aged a lifetime in a weekend but came back looking younger. Terry said he was looking forward to the funeral. He was looking forward to embracing it and moving on to the next phase of his live. He explained to me how he'd done some deep thinking and soul searching over the last week. His grandma's death had brought a lot of buried emotions to the surface. Things Terry had never been able to deal with, or have the support to deal with as a young man, now he felt confident he knew who he was. "I don't want to drink anymore Ten, I'm done with it. I'm going to AA."

I'd heard and spoken these words many times over the years. Experiencing the same gut feeling of saying 'why the fuck bother mate, you know you'll be lashed on the weekend', to being more positive, was something that was done a lot around alcoholics. I'd heard many hopeless alcoholics spit the same hopeless alcoholic lyrics year after year, as they got drunker and older but never sober. Terry was being deadly serious though. I was happy for him if that was the case. Through an almost 30 year career of drinking in pubs and bars, I would have been a millionaire if I got £1 for every alky who told me they were drying out and going to AA the next day. It was standard chat in the alky clique. A secret language you couldn't learn, you had to live it to fluently speak it. In our circle we heard these words daily. We hear the ramblings of an already distinguished hope. Clinging on to all the failures, the words are mostly practised through repetition and insincere in their delivery. The quitting alky will always need their last drink. I've sat with hundreds of alcoholics in the early stages of wet brain. I've sat and listened while nodding my head and drinking myself towards the onset of wet brain I was already experiencing. Facial twitches and body twitches became increasingly embarrassing. These guys were already there. I would be there for their last drink tonight, and I'd be there for their last drink tomorrow.

I believed Terry. I was a good judge of character and could smell bullshit from a mile away. Well, unless the stink was coming from me that is. I was always oblivious to my own brand. Terry was being sincere. Jerome came striding over, puffing his chest like a fucking gimp. He went straight over to Terry and with a smile on his face announced that Terry would not be attending his grandma's funeral, as she wasn't immediate family and service pressures would not allow. As Terry had already had unauthorized compassionate leave for those two days the union had no choice but to accept the decision. The company had the right to turn down any request. Jerome informed Terry that grandparents were not immediate family and to go and check his contract.

"Get your arse back on the phone, take some calls, service pressures are fucking ridiculous and I have to explain this shit to my bosses. If the queues are red status, I can turn down a request, and guess what fairy?

Sorry, I mean Terry. The queues are red. Granny is going to have to bury herself."

I was expecting Terry to flip out. I knew for a fact this decision would be immediately overturned anyway and Terry would attend as other people would think of their own situations and kick off. I was expecting a breakdown from Terry, tears and hysterics like I had witnesses in town while pissed up many times. He was different though, as I've said, aged a lifetime in a weekend. This wasn't 'Turbo, 10 shots of tequila and suck your cock' Terry. This was Terry 2.0. He slowly walked up to Jerome, calmly and respectfully but still with an air of menace about his movements. It wasn't apparent if Jerome was going to get a lap dance or knocked the fuck out. The closer he got the more nervous Jerome became until he was squirming where he stood like the fucking freak he was. In front of us all Terry verbally handed in his resignation.
"Stick your job Jerome, I'm too good for this place. You're a horrible human being, a mistake of the world. I don't know how poor Starr puts up with you, Jerome the gnome. Yes I've heard about your maggot dick, hardly touches the sides from what half the centre says. I bet even your mother she wishes she swallowed you. I quit, with immediate notice. Sort the paperwork, you work for me now. Bye-bye."

And with a few high 5s and handshakes and good well wishes in front of an infuriated Jerome, Terry casually strolled out of the building to bury his grandma. Terry showed the rest of us cowards how to deal with life and how to deal with bullies. He stood up to both. Both challenged him and he accepted the challenge of both. More importantly, he confidently accepted the challenge of both. Today we were taught a life lesson on how to be a man by a young man on his own in the world. I saw a man stand up to a bully and then go and bury his grandma and seek healing in the transition period himself. Without the crutch of booze. I hoped Terry would succeed and he showed me that to beat our demons, we needed to confront them head on. Then? Either make peace with them and move on. Or? Knock them the fuck out, and move on. As long as the outcome is leaving that shit in your past, and moving on, it's a good outcome. Holding onto that shit will eventually drown you.

I'd looked at myself as somewhat of a mentor to Terry, in the ways of life and drinking, as most philosophical alcoholics do, my own feeling of self-importance. Terry was actually my mentor about life, I'd been learning from him all along without even knowing it. Him talking to me for help, actually got me talking about my own issues without even thinking about it. Subconsciously Terry was counselling me and getting me to open up about my drinking. Terry had fooled me before, maybe he knew what he was doing all along, reverse psychology. Either way I'm glad he passed through my lifeline.

Chapter 32

The empty eyes that looked back at me from the mirror on the toilet roll holder, started my morning, every morning. The black holes staring back shared no signs of positivity and I felt like a pathetic loser even before I'd finished my morning shit. The new appearance of blood in my morning shit had me concerned for a few days. Not enough to stop pumping the spirits through me but enough to discuss it with Dev, Ref and Gel. Even Dev agreed we should cut down on the shorts for the time being, beer and cider only. Gel and Ref wanted full abstinence but I knew that would never work and we'd end up just arguing and giving in to Dev. A cut down was the best we could agree to at the moment. It was a compromise that Gel and Ref had no option other than to accept. We'd wait a few days and see if the blood was still there.

The blood was heavy, dark and thick. It reminded me of standing in the shower and having a three foot long, bloody, cocaine snot ball, suck your brains out through your nose and watch them escape down the plug hole. The bleeding stayed for three days and then stopped. As Dev liked to tell us quite often in the future, just as he said it would. So we didn't cut down drinking. Shitting blood was quickly forgotten about and we hammered the drink with a new gusto. We were invincible, we were the most interesting person amongst the alkies, and if you weren't amongst the alkies? It means you were not worthy enough. Who wouldn't want to hang out in all the shitty bars all day, every day, talking shit to other pissheads? They look down on us? No. We look down on you. Fuck um. They're below being graced by the barroom poet Laurette, preaching prophetical proverbs to all the pissheads and winos, who all secretly think they can match me and take my throne. But they are mistaken, because I am the king. The ridiculous thinking of my crumbling mind. I needed a change.

Chapter 33

I was born with a chip on my shoulder and I think the blood I was shitting out was the chip for the other side. I'd become a really bitter fuck. Hated my job and hated the world. I didn't want any company but I didn't want to be alone with myself all the time either. I needed a change of conversation from the seedy city bars, places where I was checking my wallet every 5 minutes. Shit holes.

After finishing an early shift, I made my way straight to the pub at 2pm. I decided to stay local and went to the pub where I first took Genevieve. I had been back many times since and the place held no demons of Genevieve for me. Those demons were stored elsewhere. I'd go back to the pub occasionally for the late night lock-ins for the pay per view boxing and poker nights but as my alcoholism spiraled out of control, I vied for anonymity and the company of strangers who I hoped I'd never meet again in most cases.

I walked into The Pendulum at about 2:20pm on a Friday and there was a fucking wake going on. GREAT!!! Be loads of people getting drunk and high early doors. I'd get involved with this. The atmosphere was surprisingly bright but as the wake was for Garry, I shouldn't have been surprised. He was a true character of the pub and someone who would have loved to be there for the following anecdote. It was his wake; no doubts Garry would have been watching over. Everyone was dressed in the customary black and whites. I was wearing jeans, a t-shirt, leather biker jacket and my Air Max but embraced by all in the place regardless of my attire. I quickly had two pints bought for me and one put behind the bar.

My entrance had not interrupted but more switched the attention from the ongoing card game. Texas Hold 'Em. Some of these games got high stakes and at those times I took my drunk ass away from the table. I'd shared the pot a few times down there but nothing of substance. The game was full anyway and there was a waiting queue of punters waiting to through their cash on the table and get involved. I was quite happy to watch the games unfold while swigging my pints and laughing at the banter as the cards were laid on the table. I loved this card game. It mirrored the wheel of life. One moment we're up, then one card flops, and we're back down in the gutter. You could be sat as small blind, holding two aces, and still leave the hand holding nothing but your balls. Alternatively, your opponent who is big blind, is sat holding a bag of shit. If he wasn't already big blind he would have folded. But he calls and carries on the game. Fucker ends up with a full house on the river card and takes the pot. Up one moment and down the next. Life. I stood behind one of the old darts players called Lester, who'd got himself a seat at the table. Lester was a funny old guy, always trying to keep up with the banter of the younger guys around the bar, many of whom had been in school with his kids and grandkids. I stood far enough back to not be influencing the game but close enough to see Lester's cards.

Mickey dealt the cards and I watched the game unfold as the room went silent. I could clearly see Lester had been dealt the 10 and King of spades. Excellent cards. The big blind was a £5 chip, small blind £2.50, and everyone called. £30 in the pot and I'd say, from previous experience, maybe £3000 at the table. There were some big players there. Lester was not rich and he was not a very good card player, but he enjoyed the company of the young crowd he'd seen grow up. Mickey deals the flop. In slow motion and causing a surreal moment in my life, I saw the Jack, Queen and Ace of spades laid on the table, one after the next. A fucking royal flush! Lester had a fucking royal flush and only he and I knew about it. The unbeatable hand. The flop had put everyone in good spirits with a lot of laughter and false tells, all good natured. But the cards are significant, these cards have made it not about cards now, but psychology.

All the players looked at each other trying to catch a glimpse of a twitch or a tell. Who was bluffing and who had the spades for a flush? Just remember someone else at the table could be holding the 8 and 9 of spades and be just as excited as Lester. The 10 and King could still be in the deck in their minds. Wow, what a situation, it was like something out of the old Wild West. As I knew Lester had already won the game it was hard to watch people throw their money down the fucking drain but that's the game. I felt empathy but I knew to keep my mouth shut, this was serious business. The next round of betting started. Mickey obviously had no sniff of a spade or pair of any kind, so bottles it. Ray places the minimum bet, a £5 chip. Lester's turn to call the bet. I'm thinking in my head, 'don't raise him Les, see his bet, don't raise it.' Lester goes all in!!! What the fuck are you doing you crazy cunt??? You've just blown a legendary hand going all in on the fucking flop! I couldn't believe it and neither could any other player at the table as they all quickly folded. I was devastated. The unbeatable hand and I was expecting some James Bond shit. The odds are 30940/1 so in all likelihood, I'd never see this happen again.

There was £40 in the pot. A once in a lifetime hand, and Lester blows it for 40 fucking pounds. If any other player at that table had the 10 and King they would have emptied the wallets and collected mortgage deeds and car keys from the other players. Lester by the rules, didn't have to show his cards after the game ended as everyone else folded. He showed them anyway. I would have too. I would have had it fucking tattooed the day later! As Lester had his Paul Newman moment and laid his cards down, everyone else around the table and at the bar sighed a collective relief and quickly emptied their glasses to much banter and shouts of another round. The drinks were served, the cigarettes were smoked and the lines were sniffed. Then, back to the table for the silence to fall as the next hand is dealt.

I walked home a few hours later, stupidly drunk. The royal flush was still fucking with my head. I get into the kitchen and slice up some limes, thickly and unevenly, for the Coronas I'd bought earlier on. The first bottle is finished quickly while sorting the music, so I drop a lime in two more and roll a joint. The flush wouldn't leave me alone as I tried to blank it out with weed smoke and alcohol. The green penetrated my brain and my drunken, self-obsessed ego found a little bit of buried empathy. Fuck knows where from. I thought out loud to myself. "What if Lester didn't lose a great opportunity? What if Lester was supposed to fuck up that hand? The Royal Flush possibly wasn't a hand destined to take money? Maybe it was to stop someone else getting taken for? Maybe it was a sign to Mickey and Ray? Or any of the other players at the table? Maybe this wasn't Lester's story? What if it was one of the other players' story? Maybe a sign for a person to change their ways after a lucky escape?"

I gently, but eagerly, pulled on the joint. Mixed with the alcohol I was stoned as fuck, real quick. Green took me to a deeper level of thinking that booze couldn't. Weed didn't hide me from myself, it showed me who I was. Whether I liked it or not. It also showed me other people's actions in a different light and context. Sometimes I realised I'd overreacted in a situation but then underreacted in others. Lessons to be learned when you look at things from a different angle. Weed was the truth teller. It showed me not everything was black and white, there's a lot of grey shit going on in life too. I got none of this from alcohol. Booze just made sure the train of misery had enough fuel in the tank for another trip round the zombie apocalypse.

In previous poker games I'd seen cards being won and lost on the tables, the flush had that vibe about it. Something special felt like it could happen, and maybe it did. But then there was nothing. An anti-climax. A great movie spoiled by a shit ending. Maybe for me. The six players at that table were involved with something that could have been life changing for them all. Cash, jewellery, cars, houses, marriages, anything could have ended up going on the table with a hand like that. Stoned and in contemplation mode I think long and hard about what I had witnesses. Maybe this wasn't any of their stories? Maybe it's mine? Maybe that royal flush was meant for me and I was just in the right place at the right time? I discussed with myself about what I really wanted to see from that game, considering I felt a great sense of disappointment from the event ending. I wondered if I would have taken pleasure in seeing someone's life destroyed in front of my eyes on the flip of a card? "Did you? Did you want to see that? Someone's life turned to shit?"

If there's a big winner there will always be big losers too in a high-stake poker game. Did I want to see someone dragged to a place to share my misery? Did I secretly yearn for someone to fuck up so bad it made me

feel better about my shitty life? I knew people who did. I knew people who did yearn for others to descend to the misery. But I didn't.
I hadn't become a fucking humanitarian but I didn't want someone to fuck their lives up so I could feel better about myself. With the third bottle finished and a forth quickly necked with the bedtime cig I headed up to bed. Drunk and stoned but happy as I fall into bed, I can feel the stupid childlike grin on my face. Even though I knew I was stoned I felt a bit of inner peace for the first time in 20 years. I felt a tiny bit of inner peace and I liked it.

Everyone from the poker game went home a little richer or a little poorer and a lot drunker. But nobody's life ruined. What I witnesses was not a once in a life time poker hand, I watched something else. I watched lives being touched and affected, even when they were not involved in the game. People in that bar had seen something that would change their thinking forever. The unbeatable hand, no legends, no myths, no bullshit, as we'd all seen it dealt in the flesh now. I went to sleep drunk and alone, but content. The royal flush story may or may not have been for me but these days I grabbed any strand of positivity on offer. A true part of myself was revealed to me and I couldn't deny it. I did have a soul. It did have a lot of fucking work to be done, but it was there. My empathy had showed me I wasn't a total cunt, it wasn't too late for me.

My soul would be tested in the coming months.

Chapter 34

The three way affair was still ongoing but for me personally, the spark was going out. It was becoming more routine than exciting, it wasn't as much fun anymore. Karley was now completely tee-total, off everything. She and her husband were planning on starting a family in the new year. Karley wanted a year to get fit and healthy after the last 15 years of being a weekend party head. I'd see her now and think of our first night together, watching boxing around my house. The pure lust and passion we had for each other back then was now completely gone. She didn't turn me on as much as she used to, and I hadn't aged well either so no doubts the feeling was mutual. Don't get me wrong, Karley still looked amazing, possibly even better than when I first met her over 10 years ago. The strains of the job had finally cracked her and she went fully corporate. Her dress sense changed along with the way she acted around the office. Even her fucking accent changed. Karley had become not just a part of the machine, she'd become a cheerleader for it. She'd become boring. Both Natasha and myself would be mothered by her about our lifestyles, even though she was actually younger than us. How we needed to calm down and stop all the drinking and drugs, blah, blah, blah. Look just because you have a perfect life and career fuck off and leave me to mine. Her words went into the head of the alcoholic and straight out. Into the head of the drug addict, and straight back out. Neither of us paid any attention to her moaning. So we tied her up and fucked her.

It was the last great night the three of us spent together. Natasha disappeared on the train back to Cardiff the next morning, this was not unusual, this was normal behaviour. We might not now have expected to see Tasha again for a few days, weeks, months, possibly years. It was how Natasha lived, she was a free spirit.

Natasha died in a Cardiff bedsit with a needle in her arm. Dreaming of being 14 again and seeing her dad, when happiness didn't come from a hit. I was deeply bitter and hurt about Natasha's death and I would constantly blame myself, but I wasn't shocked about it. We'd often joke about who would die first when it was just Tasha and me. We'd joke but we'd also have serious conversations too. Deep dark shit.

Karley had phoned me to tell me about Tasha's death, she was devastated, in complete fucking pieces. But also, eerily calm. No shouting, screaming or crying, just straight talking and a lot of regret. I struggled to put the words together as I fell on my arse, on the cold kitchen floor. I temporarily go blind as if I'm staring at the sun. my vision goes black, and then I see red and green spots jumping around as my vision returns. I don't feel I'm real. I feel like a passenger in my own body.

"Ten. She's gone babe, Tasha's gone, she's gone Ten. I can't cope with this babe, I can't cope, I can't lose Tasha. I've never loved anyone like I love Tasha, not you, not my husband, nobody. Only my Natasha. I'm sorry Natasha, I'm sorry I shouted at you the last time we spoke, please forgive me, I'm so sorry, I love you so much my Natasha." I'd already broken down into tears as I heard my friend and my lover lose the most important person she'd ever had in her life. What Tasha and I had was nothing like the love between those two had for each other. Soulmates who drifted in and out of each other's lives constantly since they were 18 years old, but a couple that I'm convinced would have been together until something like this separated them. I couldn't imagine the pain Karley was feeling.

After there was nothing else to be said or done on the phone Karley informed me that she would be taking time off work before the funeral. I wouldn't see her until then. I tell Karley that Natasha loved her deeply. My remark is not given a response. Karley tells me she will let me know of the funeral plans and ends the call.

Sat on the kitchen floor and I can't stop crying. I take off all my clothes and put them in the washing machine and put an hour wash on. I sit naked on the cold ground, drunkenly swigging from three different bottles of spirits, crying while I talk to Natasha, while I watch our souls get clean. I'm drunk and I want another fucking cycle, so I put the clothes to go around again. I want more time.

Drinking on the floor in front of the washing machine I'm hypnotized by the movements and sounds. I'm transported to a higher dimension where for a brief second the whole world makes sense. Every little bit, every little detail. It's all explained, including my life. And then, the thought process disappears, and I forget everything I ever knew. Natasha would go away until she got bored. Then she'd return. She'd go away. Then come back some other time. Maybe hiding but always running, Natasha never stopped anywhere for long. Tasha was a slave to the misery, just like me. She knew how to get rid of the misery but didn't want to. It made her happy knowing the misery was still there if she needed it, if the fear got too much. Tasha didn't want the misery but couldn't live without it.

It's still here Tasha, the misery, it's always here babe, but not for you anymore. Sleep tight my crazy little succubus, those hellhounds ain't chasing you no more xxx

Chapter 35

The funeral was at midday on the outskirts of Cardiff. I think it was a Tuesday. Luckily the only suit I owned was dark and I'd borrowed a black tie from a drinking buddy down the boozer. When Karley turned up to pick me up I looked like a bag of shit.
"Look at the state of you babe, you look like shit."
Karley's tone was not one of anger or disappointment, it was more of concern. In her heart of hearts, she always thought I'd be the one to drink myself to death or overdose, not Natasha. All three of us did. Karley knew I wasn't far off joining Tasha myself, but I was oblivious to the obvious.

After coming in the house to scrub me up to look more presentable, we both end up in tears. The pain I see from Karley is like nothing I've ever seen before. I was reduced to an emotional jellyfish as Karley's face contorted and screamed in pain, as if being tortured on some medieval device. I could see her soul being ripped apart. I could hear it, feel it. I could fucking touch it. I was terrified of that hurt. I hoped I never found love again to be put through that. I held Karley tight to my chest as we silently embraced for what seemed like only a minute or two, but was closer to an hour. After cleaning our faces and smoking a cigarette we made the 45-minute drive. Karley drove and stayed silent the entire journey. We arrived at the church and parked close by. The street was quiet and the day was cold, but it was bright. We approached the large wooden doors and still hadn't seen anyone yet. As the door opened, we saw a few of Tasha's friends who seemed genuinely upset. There were three Somalian guys stood over to the side who turned out to be associates of Natasha's late father, there to pay their respects.

Without warning, from behind me I felt the presence of something big and imposing. And then came the voice.
"No fucking drinking in here Swansea boy, I've been told about you."
With the strongest Welsh valleys accent I'd heard in a while I turned around to see 6'4 and 250lbs of Tongan muscle, staring intimidatingly down at me. Now, I could ruck a little bit, but I wasn't suicidal. I was shitting myself at the prospect of having to fight this fucking guy. He carried on speaking. "But Tash said you were a good guy and I could tell when Tash knew a good one was a good one. It's a pity you don't think that son, look at the fucking state of you man, when's the last time you ate?"

The infamous Uncle Mus. He took me outside for a chat and we went round the back of the church where Uncle Mus gave me a sandwich and a can of lager from his car. I was told I wasn't a bad person, I was told not to carry on punishing myself for something in my past, something I no longer had any control over. I was told to forgive everyone of their sins towards me. I was told to forgive myself. I was told I would find my true self one day and become a spiritual person. I was told I would be reborn. The infamous Uncle Mus. When we went back in Karley was being consoled by Auntie Jo, who was more like a mother to Tasha than her real mum ever was, Jo was Tasha's dad's sister. The service began and it was over quickly, it was a traditional service which Tasha would have hated. I exchanged some small talk with the Somalian fellas and a few other mourners before Karley and I decided to make a move. Neither of us could face going to the wake which was in a city centre pub. Auntie Jo and Uncle Mus were swerving it as well, they knew some of Tasha's crazy party friends and junkies would be there, along with Tasha's mother.

Natasha's mother did not attend the funeral, she stayed in the pub, while Auntie Jo and Uncle Mus buried her daughter two miles down the road. Tasha's mum went to the pub to immerse herself in all the love, sympathy, support, and free drinks lavished on her from total strangers. She hadn't seen Natasha in six years. Karley had met her and had nothing good to say about her. I had no desire to meet the woman.

Uncle Mus grabbed my phone and punched in his number with his giant hands. He handed the phone back to me and as he did he grabbed me with both arms and hugged me. "You're lost Ten, you're lost son. You got my number and I'll text you my address later. Get the fuck out of Swansea for a bit son, come and stay with me and Jo. We got a nice house in a nice area, some tranquility for you." Uncle Mus was convinced he was talking to a dead man, unless I changed my ways soon. He didn't pull any punches and hit me with some home truths that hurt more than any punch I ever took in the boxing ring or in the street. "When I was your age Ten I was given seven years in prison. I was out by my early 40s and my life is good. It can be for you too, just knock all that shit on the head, you hear me boy? The drink, the fucking drugs, they're killing you. You're still young enough to leave this shit behind and make a good life for yourself. The misery only stays as long as you let it Ten.''

Even though it was the first time I met them and they weren't my family, I addresses both as Auntie Jo and Uncle Mus from the start. After our first exchange of words it felt comfortable, it felt right. Auntie Jo kissed my cheek and then held my face while looking deep into my eyes. She stared softly for more than a few moments.
"My poor boy. What are you doing to yourself? What things you have seen, the universe has a plan for you my son, just be patient.''
I broke down into her arms as she cradled my head against her soft shoulder. Natasha had told me about her dad and Auntie Jo's upbringing in Somalia and some of the atrocities they had seen, things I found hard to put into words. If we were playing 'shit lives top trumps' Auntie Jo would beat you hands down. She had the Buggati of shit lives. This wonderful woman who had seen and been through so much. A woman who buried the closest thing she had to a daughter, and the closest thing that daughter had to a mum, less than 30 minutes ago. This woman was cradling an alcoholic thug in her arms, who was also a stranger, telling him the universe had a plan for him and he'd be ok. Unbelievable. I felt like a child.

Karley walked Auntie Jo to her car and I followed with Uncle Mus as we talked about the previous weekend's boxing, I enjoyed his company even on such a tragic day. He pulled me to one side and we smoked a cigarette while Uncle Mus spoke.
"Someone like you gets more out of life once you slow down. You're a fucking wild horse, trying to drink and fuck everything moving. Can't be doing that forever boy. Sort your fucking shit out son, or I'll come to Swansea and sort you myself.'' The words were the first to ever really touch me, as Uncle Mus had spoken to me in a little detail about his

own struggle with booze. He could see the similarities in us and the shit that goes on behind the eyes, the anger, the hate. Uncle Mus could see it. He could see me.

"You may think this is all you were born for Ten, where you belong? It's not. This fucking drinking life man, it's no good, it's got a shelf life. First it'll take your life. And then it will kill you." As we parted ways Uncle Mus shouted over that he'd be texting to check in from time to time, I told him no problem as we waved them off.

"First it takes your life, then it kills you. Fucking hell." Karley looked on concerned.
"What does that mean babe? Are you ok?"
"Yeah I'm good babe. I think he was a fisherman. Deep man babe, deep, deep man. Let's go home."

Chapter 36

Karley sat in the passenger seat of her car and I drove back. I didn't fancy being alone with my own thoughts and the boredom of the M4 did appeal either. I headed through the valleys, Karley was staying with me tonight so we were in no rush to get home. Driving through the valleys it became blatantly obvious that South Wales likes a drink, fuck me I seen some crazy cunts while Karley dozed in and out of sleep. All the crying and emotions had taken it out of her and she was exhausted. The more people I saw drunk in the street, the more I identified with them, and I didn't like it. Alcoholics, deep down, always feel alone. Which is strange as we are probably part of the world's biggest and most ethnically diverse social group, spawned over every race, religion, gender on the planet. In a world where greed is king and the rich/poor divide gets wider every day, most talking heads we see on TV may say the right things, but we still don't believe them. The only true empathy a poor person will get from a rich person is if they're alcoholic. It's the only thing in life that is able to put us all on the same level, the equalizer, the final say.

A millionaire junkie can never empathize with a street junkie, not even the craving, even that's different, as money makes it different. The millionaire probably won't have to suck someone's cock for a hit if they needed one. They look at the street junkies as scum, they don't share any identification with them, not even the drug, or the craving, or the hit. A billionaire alcoholic can be walking down the street, with their 12 security guys all tooled up and walk past a homeless alcoholic sat on the street drinking a can of Tennent's Super 9%. The billionaire alcoholic will see the drunk, see the alcohol, and identify immediately. They identify with the struggle rather than the person, they identify with the alcohol and all the similarities it ingrains in us. And then they go down the corner shop with their security crew, and buy up all the Frosty Jacks white cider off the shelf, then go and get drunk as fuck in the park!

We stayed out driving until it got dark and picked up some food on the way home. We ate and drank well while listening to music and having a few meaningless conversations about nothing. It wasn't awkward, it was just ending. "Ten I want to go to bed, will you come to bed with me please babe?"

Karley led me up the stairs and we had sex on the bed, but there was no passion, it was more ritualistic. We were going through Tasha's death. The end of the three way affair. The end of the separate affairs we had with Tasha. The end of whatever it was me and Karley had. It was the final fuck. Karley fell asleep on my chest, gently weeping. I just lay there holding her, I was all cried out.

I made fresh coffee early the next morning and smoked cigarettes in my kitchen, while Karley was still asleep in my bed. I wasn't feeling anxious even though I was chain smoking rollies and drinking loads of coffee, a weight had felt lifted a little. The fate of the inevitable was something I had to embrace. A new start, quit drinking, maybe even a new job?

I heard Karley get up and have a shower. I'd had one a couple of hours before and wanted to not look like a bag of shit so I'd put on some jeans and a shirt, rather than my house drinking attire consisting of trackies and t-shirts. Karley walked down the stairs and I poured a fresh cup of coffee and left it on the side for her as she walked in. I handed her a cigarette I'd already rolled.

"No thanks babe. I know I was smoking yesterday but I needed to, or I wouldn't have been able to cope. I've quit babe, quit everything. I want a baby Ten."

"You'll make a great mother babe, I know it."

Karley held both of my hands.

"Let's call it a day babe? Now Tasha's gone I'm going to try and make my marriage work. I want kids Ten and I'm sober now. I was already going in a different direction from you and Natasha, this isn't my life anymore Ten. I'm a wife and I want to be a mother, I'm sorry babe."

I already knew it was coming but I was surprised at how relived I was that the end was here. The only reason the affair had been going for the last few years was Tasha. Both Karley and myself enjoyed our solo time with Natasha more than the three of us together, but Tasha loved the trio. In the end I fucked Karley to fuck Tasha, and Karley did the same.

"You're right babe, I completely agree with you. It's what Tasha would have wanted, she always said you'd be a great mother one day. It's what I want too babe." That was true. I thought about my words before I spoke the truth. She looked sad and happy at the same time, until it dawned on her, and she broke down. "Over 10 years babe, it's been over 10 years." She was right. We'd been sleeping with each other for over 10 years. We started our relationship before she'd even met her fucking husband. It was a bigger deal than Karley had expected as she lost control of her strawberry like lips as they quivered in rhythm with her weeps. Such a beautiful woman. I grab her and pull her into my chest and can feel her heart beating against mine. We hold each other and talk. We talk about the next steps to take as I'm informed Karley will be moving out of Wales. Her notice was already handed in and outstanding holiday hours owed means she will never return the call centre.

"I want this to be our final contact Ten, a clean break. No phone, no Facebook, no contact whatsoever, ever again. It ends today babe." I wholeheartedly agreed with Karley but I was still getting the vibe she was trying to convince herself and not me. She carried on. "You and Natasha will always be a part of my history. Some of the greatest moments of my life, and the most fun I've ever had, were the three of us. I can never change that and would never want to. But if I want a future I need to leave my past where it is."

She went on to say how she'd always love Natasha and love me as well. We share a final hug and one last passionate kiss, that reminds me of the first time we got together, it reminds Karley too. We have a final laugh at our sudden burst of passion and what dirty dogs we were a decade ago. I see that carefree spirit and laughter from her I haven't seen in years, it's nice to see that person is still there as I've missed her. Just like Auntie Jo had done, Karley puts both hands on my face and plants a kiss on my forehead. "Please don't die babe, you need help, you're not a well person Tennyson. I want you to live. Even though this is it for us, it will be comforting for me to know you're still in the world." I tell her I will seek out help, but I have no real intention. Uncle Mus' words still hadn't fully processed in my junkyard of a brain. Those words would slow cook for another couple of years before I was ready to use them.

Natasha had told Karley she was in love with me and about our affair. Karley tells me she's glad Natasha had me in her life, as she couldn't be there for her all the time herself. She tells me she loves me as well, always has and always will, but not as a husband or father to her child. "I know babe, I love you too and I'll always love Tasha. I'll never forget either of you." I spoke the truth when I said I'd never forget them but I lied when I said I loved them. I did love them but not like I loved Genevieve, nowhere near. I'd had great times with Karley for over 10 years and I had love for her. I'd enjoyed even better times with Natasha over a shorter period of time and I had even more love for Tasha. But ultimately, I never really loved either. I didn't want Karley's final moments with me to portray any negativity, we'd shared too much to let the truth ruin it. Our nerves were still raw and Karley deserved to be lied to. It was the right thing to do.

"Please don't come to the car Ten, stay here, let me remember how you were when I first turned up here for the boxing. I want to remember the last time I see you to be stood in the door of the house we had such great times in. And that includes the times before I even introduced Tasha to you Wilde boy."
Karley giggled a little and gave me a kiss on the lips and left with the parting words.

"I always loved the sex life I had with you babe but I was jealous of what you and Tasha had without me."
"We had the misery babe. That's all. She got the love from you and the misery with me. She needed us both."
"My handsome boy. Thank you Tennyson."

Karley walked to her car and didn't look back. She started the engine and slowly drove down my street, looking in her rear view mirror as I watched her disappear out of sight forever.

Chapter 37

Shitty streets as the city weeps, the tears on the road reflecting the street lights to guide me home. Every footstep I take is sound tracked by a gentle splash, as I deftly dodge the dogshit deliberately left by some cunt from up the road. It's mostly quiet and peaceful apart from the occasional diesel engine which you hope is a taxi and not the old bill to pull you. I get home, drunk and wet as I climb into bed.

I return to work the next day, badly hungover, even by my standards. I think I'm passed caring. I'd used up all my sick days and compassionate leave I'd made up over the year. All the emergency days and family days used on hangovers. Another unauthorized absence would result in a 'fact finding' session, which was basically an hour long interview to break down how shit your performance has been. This interview would be conducted by my line manager and also theirs. That meant Jerome and Jacqui. These two motherfuckers were still having an affair behind Starr's back. This kind woman, who only 8 or 9 years ago would babysit Jacqui as a favour to her friend who was Jacqui's mum. The thought of being interviewed by these two snakes as they played footsie under the table made me sick. I would have rather done a full day on the phones hungover to fuck than spend even 10 minutes with those two Kentucky fried cunts. I'd literally done thousands of days hungover on the phones over 12 years, I could easily do another one.

As we got ready to take calls we get a loud shout from Jacqui, "EVERYBODY, check your emails immediately please."
This normally meant we had some sort of meaningless task to complete online, so I'd normally ignore it until I got a reminder, usually months down the line.
"Tennyson. Did you read the email?" Knowing full well I hadn't as she had access to our inbox, I answered her.

"I'll read it in a bit Jac, I'm busy with a customer at the moment." But Jacqui was adamant. She wanted it read now.
"Alright Jac, gimme a minute, let me look."

'TEAM MEETING, 2:30PM, ROOM 8'

And that was it.
"Fucking hell Jac was it really a requirement to email us all? Why didn't you just tell us?"
"Yes Ten I needed to email you all so you could put it in your electronic calendars."
"Why didn't you just say, team meeting at 2.30, room 8, don't be late. Instead of doing cryptic shit and tell us to check our fucking emails."
I sat and looked at her while I awaited her answer.
"Well Tennyson, if I said it out loud not everyone might have heard me and I'd have to repeat it. This will save time and save the bank money in the long run. An email is the most cost effective way of communicating within the workplace."
Glug had joined in now,
"What? More cost effective than telling us verbally?"
"Yes Richard."
"Are you being fucking serious?"
"Richard please remember where you are and the company's core standards, please watch your language."
"This place is fucking banana's son."
"Why do you say that Richard?"
"Well if email is the most cost effective way of communication, why do you insist on visiting Jerome's desk every 10 minutes?"
"Back on the phones please Richard."

2:30 couldn't come quick enough. The meeting would last until 4pm which was my clocking off time. I'd zone out in the meeting and drink coffee while having silent conversations in my head with the voices about how much we planned on drinking that night to nurse this hangover. I'd stopped speaking in team meetings as I found that whenever I would open my mouth, I normally ended up dropping myself in the shit. I'd previously been a little aggressive in putting my point forward about workers' rights and I'd been reported to HR for my 'intimidating behaviour'. I just didn't like having a spineless manager who wouldn't stick up for themselves or their workers, it pissed me off, so I would just sit there silent and nod my head in agreement until 4pm.

The first half of the meeting was boring procedural shit that nobody had a clue about, including the person stitched up to deliver the training. After the presentation they would send an email of all the slides and if we had any questions to email. The room was small and cramped and we were all sat close together. Jess, Pacman, Marie, Glug, Sadie, Mario, me, Barnsey, and Jacqui. Then in walks Jerome. Nobody even hid the contempt anymore as there was a collective sigh as we'd have to listen to this bell end for the next 45 minutes. He even flirted with Jacqui as soon as he came in and made a point of sitting next to her and stroking her leg. Glug had had enough.
He told Jerome and Jacqui.
"That shit is out of order. Your wife is 50 feet down the corridor from us, show us some respect as workers and friends of Starr. I don't want to see that shady shit."
Jerome fired back without a pause.
"Well if you like that Glug you'll love that we are cutting your two 15 minute breaks to two 10 minute breaks. The bank has determined that 10 minutes away from the screen is more than enough time for a break. A shorter break will also make you work more efficiently as you will have 5 minutes less time to fall out of character." Glug didn't even wait for Jerome to finish as he stood up and pointed directly in Jerome's face.

"You're a fucking cocksucker pal, always trying to fuck us over. You've fucked loads of people over in this place, you fucked Morgan over, you've fucked Starr over and now you're fucking us over too."
I don't know how drunk Glug was but he was definitely on the wrong side of slurred speech pattern.

"Starr deserves better than you, you creep. This is what she deserves!" Glug fumbles at his trousers and then whips out what can only be described as a fucking huge cock. I don't know what the fuck he had been doing to the poor fucker though, it was battered, it looked like Sylvester Stallone at the end of Rocky II.

"This is what Starr deserves, you tell her Jerome, you tell her it's here waiting. Girls, tell Starr to come see me. I'll ruin her whenever she wants more than chipolata dick Jerome. I quit cunt, I'm going down the pub." Glug used both hands to put his dick back in his pants, while at the same time telling a jaw dropped Jerome. "I'm gonna fuck your wife mate and she's gonna love it." And with that Glug walked out of the centre and never returned. As everyone sat there astonished at what we had just seen, Mario is the first to make a comment in his broken English.

"I told you Glug got that pornstar dick man, fucking beast dick. Jerome if Glug stick that thing in Starr your little dick never touch the sides of her pussy again man." We all roared with laughter, including Jacqui, as Jerome stormed out of the room and straight to call the police on Glug. When the police caught up with Glug a few days later he was charged with indecent exposure. He pleaded guilty and was sentenced to 150 hours community service and a £200 fine. How the fuck he never went to prison I'll never know, especially after he gave the judge a piece of his mind.

"Look judge. Send me down if you want, I don't care. I got loads of mates who've done time and some still inside now. They love it, say it's like the last day of school every day. You get to play games and fuck around with your mates all day. A kid off my street is in Parc Prison right now, fucker got to take his Xbox with him.''

Glug didn't go to jail but he did go into business once his community service was done. A talented artist, Glug would do some amazing custom tattoo designs that were out of this world. He would go on to get an exclusive client base that included a few famous local faces and hundreds of new customers willing to pay good money just for the design. I'd known Glug for well over a decade and I would miss his company and leftfield conversations. The boring, corporate, monotonous day job we inhabited for 8 hours a day had finally pushed even a stoner like Glug to snapping point. The atmosphere on the team was never the same once Glug went. The heartbeat of the team had been removed. Slowly but surely everyone I had known for years, the 'long termers' started to leave. Some were gone by choice, others were sacked, others were managed out. If they wanted you out, you would be gone within two weeks. Being managed out basically meant you would be spied on 100% of the time for 100% of your calls. When enough fuck ups had been detected there would be a performance review, which would always end up with a gross misconduct case pending due to something said or done on the phone. This was unfair as if everyone had their calls listened to all week, we'd all be fucking sacked. They could choose who they wanted to 'manage' out, it was an easy process. They'd send you home while they investigate and then you'd get a phone call to say don't bother coming back, P45 is in the post.

All week we'd been told we were having important visitors, which just meant we would have some rich cunts from London come up and look at us like zoo animals. They'd tell us what a great job we were doing, how we were the backbone of the bank, how we were the banks most important employees (and lowest paid), blah blah blah. Usual jobsworth shit from a cunt on a seven figure salary. This particular cunt was called David Nash and he was a seven figure salary cunt too, very high up on the food chain in this place. All the managers were making a fuss and telling us to behave ourselves, don't moan about our jobs or the customers, don't be negative, and don't act like twats, the big boss is here.

Pacman and I were walking back down the centre from our first 10 minute cigarette break when we saw Jerome approaching with David Nash. Jerome was being fake as fuck and kissing ass, being nice and friendly to people he would normal put down. As Pacman and myself approached I heard Jerome proclaim.
"Here come two of the center's top performers Mr Nash, Tennyson and Liam. Guys, come here and say hello to Mr Nash."
Pacman listened less than I did and he had no fucking clue who Mr Nash was. Without warning or hesitation, Pacman dived straight in and started talking to this guy as if he was one of Pacman's weekend drinking buddies.

"Alright Nashy boy, what's happening son?" Jerome went fucking pale as Pacman started reeling off stories to 'Nashy boy' about all the stuff we got up to and the shit we would give customers.
"Right Nashy boy, I better get back on the phone son, don't want chipolata dick Jerome on my ass."
I couldn't believe what I just saw, I still hadn't said a word for about three minutes, I was fucking dumbstruck but also laughing my ass off inside. Jerome sent Jacqui the email that Pacman's performance would need to be 'managed'. He was out of the bank in less than two weeks. Sadie handed in her notice and left with Pacman. I'd now lost three good friends in as many weeks, trustworthy friends. I was one of the

143

dying breeds, a sales rep blagging a job as a script reader, they wanted us dinosaurs gone.

The centre wanted fresh meat and people who would do as they were told and not think for themselves. Free thinking was frowned upon. They wanted young people they could mould and manipulate, to be what they wanted them to be. To not be us. I was very much alone and I could feel the vultures circling. I was on borrowed time and had no real mates I could trust anymore to keep an eye out for me, or give me a heads up when shit was about to go sour. I was where I was 12 years ago, only a little fatter, a little older, a little drunker and a lot lonelier.

Chapter 38

Booze and drugs were the wrong medicine for the illness I had, but they were the only things that would make me feel better. They were the only things that made me feel, something. The universe was putting me through all this shit just so I had something to write about. Our dark sides will eventually show themselves once alcohol is introduced to the party. After a while the person that was there is eroded away by the alcohol, like the cliffs down at Beachy Head being eroded by the sea. They become extinct and the savage emerges to become the permanent face to the problem. But I'm not blaming alcohol. Blaming alcohol for my illness is like blaming the brick that you've just thrown through somebody's window. The brick did what it was supposed to do, I can't blame the brick. The booze did the same.

Alcoholism was not my illness; it was my symptom. It should have been an indicator, that there was a deeper mental illness affecting me, but instead it just became my life crutch to forget I actually had an illness. I was ultimately trying to drink myself to death and I still didn't know why? I was drunk five days out of seven for the last ten years, shitfaced for the other two. I was suffering from a spiritual malady with a broken mind, it was a damaged and dangerous place to be imprisoned. I was a man searching for a meaning while at the same time, living a meaningless existence. I felt isolated from the world and every individual in it. I wasn't suicidal but I didn't care much for living anymore. Work had become a place I dreaded going every day. I fucking hated the job. Each morning I would need to stop myself coming up with an excuse to phone in sick, it was getting out of control. Now in my mid 30s, every hangover became a bad one. The occasional blackouts I would suffer now happened 100% of the time I drank more than a few cans. I started blacking out when I was not completely drunk and I noticed my speech would slur, again when I was 'sober'. The symptoms of 'wet brain' were apparent and I'd also started to develop facial and body twitches that were embarrassing. I stopped going out drinking and instead would drink myself to oblivion in my house every night. I had little use of friends as by this point I didn't like any cunt anyway, including myself.

I was one of the old dogs in the centre now. I'd seen people I joined with go into their 30s, their 40s, their 50s, their 60s. Individuals I'd first met in their mid 20s now coming up to their 40th birthday, I'd seen people age a lifetime right before my eyes. I'd started exercising a little more but refused to cut down on the booze, I still thought I was a 21-year-old sailor and not an alcoholic coming up to midlife. I was pushing my body to the limits it no longer had the capabilities of reaching and the mixture of booze and exercising was confusing it. I long since stopped eating regularly, one meal a day if I could manage it. I was more inclined to get the calories and hydration I needed straight from the beer and shorts. I was now constantly twitching and shaking after a few hours without alcohol, and sleep was impossible unless I was completely shit faced.

The ongoing affair between Jerome and Jacqui had been going on for so long that many of the younger, new employees, actually respected their commitment. I heard people praising their behaviour and how cute it was. And yes, these people were well aware of Starr and where she worked, they simply didn't give a fuck. In a society now obsessed with celebrity, social media, and reality TV, everyone in the world became an expert on being a fucking minge. The annual work's award ceremony was always held somewhere posh and expensive. It was an invitation only event, black tie shit. I got invited a couple of times, when mis-selling was celebrated as a good thing. As soon as they took my balls off me on the phones I never got invited again, my performances dropped. I turned the two invitations down, not my scene.

After every show there would be photos sent around of the winners getting their prizes, big screens and shit, lights, cameras, no expense spared. A carnival of narcissism. When the email was sent three days later, it was sent to every employee of the company in the world. Of the 30 or so photos at least double figures had Jerome and Jacqui all over each other like teenagers at a fucking prom. It was sickening, I was fucking disgusted and felt so sorry for Starr. It's hard to put into words what a lovely person Starr was, and even though it doesn't make a difference, she was a fucking stunningly attractive lady as well, great body, fit as fuck.

The photos quickly found their way to social media, where the likes and comments hit the 100 mark within an hour. I read the comments and I was glad I did.
"You look great together."
"When's the wedding?"
"Bet the sheets were a mess in the morning!"
"Did you do her up the tradesman entrance?"
"What a great looking couple."
"So in love xxx"

"I bet he didn't touch the sides!"

On and on the comments went. Some of the comments being left were by people I actually liked and thought were ok. I felt a little let down, as I wiped people from my mental chalkboard of individuals I could trust in work. My board wasn't far off empty after this latest episode. These two slags were reveling in the attention, it went straight to their already overinflated egos. I could see that Starr was online too, watching this all unfold to the world. Pictures were edited and shared all over the place and it was fucking everywhere. Starr sat in her office down the hall crying as her husband changed his social media status from 'married' to 'in a relationship' with Jacqui. It was the final kick in the guts from Jerome as he ended his marriage in front of an audience of cheerleaders and dickheads.

The center's new golden couple paraded around the floor taking great delight in accepting congratulations, high fives and all types of other shit from people whose gums I would now not piss on even if their teeth were on fire. If shitting in their mouth would save their lives, I'd hold that fucker in. People so inbred they're almost a fucking sandwich. Motherfuckers so up their own asses that if I wanted to kill myself I'd climb their egos and leap to their IQ. A bunch of people whose fathers should have sprayed them over their mother's tits instead. I hardly ever experienced the feeling of empathy anymore, but the situation with Starr upset me. Another case of a good person getting shit on by life while others dodge the karma bullet, time and time again. It didn't seem fair. It wasn't fair. Starr went straight to HR and informed of her intention to leave immediately, she couldn't work for this company anymore. Tony was a good guy who worked in HR, he told Starr to go home and he'd sort the absence with her manager.

"I'll pencil you in as off work for the next few days Starr. Go home and have a think. If you still want to leave, give me a call and I'll sort it."

Tony was as good as his word when Starr called up two days later confirming her decision to quit. By the end of the day her one month's notice was emailed in to Tony and he put her on 'gardening leave' for the rest of her notice period. Starr never returned to the centre. She went home, packed her shit, and moved out. She found the courage to be strong, she also found something else. A dilemma.

Chapter 39

This hangover felt different. My alarm went off at 6:30am and I dragged my drunken carcass to the toilet for an always emotional morning shit after a night on the lash. I sat on the shitter and turned my head to the right to see my disgrace of a face in the toilet roll mirror. I don't know what I expected to see but it didn't surprise me too much anymore. I was still fucked up and quite drunk, more than most mornings. I could feel my stomach turning and through experience knew I had about 15 seconds before I'd be spewing. Naked and shitty on both knees, praying to the shit sprayed bowl. I started throwing up big chunks of nothing but I was still retching. My throat and stomach started to burn as the taste in my mouth turned bitter and acidy. I retched up yellow and black bile while my throat burned, the heaving continued. I'd done this thousands of times over the years but never with such intensity. This was new. At one point I seriously thought I'd spewed an internal organ, I was fucked. But the pain started to subside so I wiped my ass and jumped in the shower.

I sipped a pint of water in the darkness of my living room, where only four hours before I was drinking rum and sniffing shit cocaine. The remnants of the night before surrounded me, as I used an empty sleeve of rizla to scrape together a line of coke left from the dust on the case of my Jimmy Cliff CD. It was no rockstar line but it gave me a little buzz to get my shit together, have a quick tidy up and walk to work. The walk was cold and peaceful while the fresh air was doing a good job of clearing my head. By the time I got to work I felt alright. Hungover, but I'd had 10 times worse than this so I got on the phones and hoped the day would go quick.

By about 2pm I started getting pains in my lower back. I thought I just needed another shit and that would sort the pain, so I left my desk and strolled off to the toilets, head down as I didn't want to talk to anyone. After a few minutes of sitting on the toilet it was obvious I didn't need a shit. I was already fucking empty from this morning, and still hadn't eaten all day. I was hot and sweaty in February and I didn't feel well. My old boss Leighton who was now on another team seen me walking back to my desk.

"Fucking hell Wildey boy, you ok? You look like shit."
I think Late thought this was a standard hangover and expecting a bit of banter in return but he seen the look of sheer desperation and fear in my face.
"You need to go home Ten, you don't look good. You need someone to drive you home?"
Late had known me long enough to know I wasn't a blagger, he knew when I was hungover and he knew when it was something else.
"Fucking go home Ten, leave it with me. Text me when you're home and if you feel like shit tomorrow just text me again and I'll sort your sickie for you."
"Thanks Late, I feel fucking horrible mate, really bad, I'll text you later."

I grabbed my stuff and hot footed out of the door as quick as I could. By the time I'd reached the main road I was doubled up in agony on the side of the road as cars went passed. The pain in my back was unbearable and on top of that I could now feel a headache brewing. But this one was coming on quick, second by second quick. Within 90 seconds I was sat on the rain soaked pavement with hands either side of my head trying to hold it together, I could feel it splitting in half. I couldn't stay still as it hurt and I couldn't move as it hurt. I didn't know what the fuck to do so I got a quick march on the go and ploughed home quickly.

I managed to get home but it wasn't quick, it took over double the usual time and the pain was getting worse. Bad thoughts started racing through my mind and I was now genuinely afraid. I grab my car keys and run to the car but the pain is so severe I can't even face turning the key, let alone drive to hospital in rush hour traffic. I can't stand, sit, lie down, nowhere I go is comfortable. The pain is the boss, and I am its bitch. The electric shock sensations in my head moved slowly up my face and through my eye, over my forehead and then like a sandcastle on the beach, the pain washes over me and I fail to exist with the living. I kept thinking of all my tattoos and the pain they caused, the boxing matches and barroom brawls, glassings and overdoses. I'd been through much worse I said to myself. I hadn't. Nothing came remotely close to this pain. I would scream in agony as another wave of destruction rips through my head as I'm curled up on the floor like a fucking new born baby.
"Fuck this, I'm calling an ambulance."

And within 30 minutes I'm stood in the doorway of my house, twisting and cavorting like Mick fucking Jagger, stripped to the waist. I'm begging the paramedics to help me, screaming in pain. They can see I'm not injured or drunk so they immediately think I'm having some sort of mental breakdown. I'm freezing cold but wearing clothes makes the pain worse, fuck knows why. Taking them off hasn't helped much either. I walk into my living room as the paramedics follow me in. I lie on the sofa, writhing in pain as I shield my eyes.
"What have you taken Tennyson?"
That was a fair question I thought, considering the state I was in. But unfortunately, I was in no fit state to give a fair answer.

"Fuck all, I swear, I haven't taken anything today. I was in work and the pain started, it's coming back, fuck no, stop it, fuck dying, take the pain away, I don't want it." I was glad I'd sniffed the rest of the coke and cleared the empty cans and bottles away before work, it wouldn't have looked good on the paramedic's report. I didn't want alcohol to take the blame because I was too soft to take an ass whooping.

"Ok Tennyson, we're just going to take your blood pressure."
It took one paramedic to hold me still and the other one to do the procedure. I was frantic, scared and in more pain than I thought was possible for the human body to take. Luckily at this point I didn't know it would get worse, the thought of that might have been enough to finish me off. The paramedics were now concerned after the blood pressure results and quickly bundled me into the ambulance and pumped me full of painkillers but wouldn't let me suck on the Entonox gas. It took fucking ages to get to the hospital even though we had the lights and sirens on. The painkillers had done fuck all and the pain was bounding in and out as I found myself slipping in and out of consciousness, I was fucking tired.

"Give me drugs doc, I can't stand this. Give me anything, I don't care, just fucking knock me out doc." I crawled and squirmed on the floor in front of the young doctor as he looked at me while taking notes. Then he disappeared.
"Where you going? Doc, where the fuck you going? I'm dying doc, gimme some drugs doc." I got up off the floor and started walking bare chested around the emergency room, begging for help, asking for a doctor. I considered trying to knock myself out with a punch or smashing my head against the wall but the pain I was already experiencing made me think any more collision to my head and I'd fucking die. Fear had taken over the controls in my brain.
The doctor came back in and I could tell by his face he thought I was a junkie. I wasn't.

He gave me a big white capsule and told me to stick it up my arse. I normally would have questioned this but at the time I didn't give a fuck and rammed it up my arse. He then gave me two different pills to swallow which I would have preferred he gave me first as my hand now stank of ass crack. I could feel the capsule melting in my arsehole and hoped the ones in my belly were quickly doing the same. I kept thinking I was shitting myself with the sensation of the arse pill. The other two kicked in and after about three hours of hell, I felt a calming sensation. The pain was gone but I felt strange, vulnerable and alone. I felt real fear and I was scared shitless.

After a few hours they moved me to a ward where they wanted to do more tests in the morning. They pumped me full of drugs and I drifted into as beautiful painless haze. When I awoke a few hours later the pain was gone. Well, the physical pain was gone but I was still tortured by the mental anguish. I looked around at things and touched what was in arms distance just to make sure I was awake. I wanted to feel something tangible after spending all day fighting an invisible opponent. I was hungry as fuck too. I asked one of the nurses for something to eat and was brought a chicken mayo baguette and a small bottle of orange juice. I thanked the nurse and tucked into my first food in days. As the food was devoured like an animal, I felt the fear return. I could sense another bout with the invisible opponent was looming and another few hours in hell. I couldn't take it again. The panic kicked in quickly.
"No, no, no, not again please, I can't take it again, please stop."
But it was too late, the wave had already broken and my pleas were pointless. Here it comes.
"No, fuck no, no, nurse, NUUUURRRSSSEEE!!!"

The pain came back with a vengeance and it wasn't fucking around with foreplay. I was about to get skull fucked without even having my balls tickled first. It was the only time I'd ever seriously considered suicide. Not so much considered but thought it was the only way out, the lesser of two evils. I searched around the bed for anything and if there was a gun close to hand I can safely say I would not have thought twice about blowing my fucking head off. Two nurses who were stationed in the corridor came running in to find me already on my hands and knees with my arse showing from the gown for all the world to see. I couldn't stay still for long enough to get my blood pressure taken, the pain was worse this time. More intense, quicker, and uglier. I was holding my head together again as it slowly and painfully split in half. I felt as if my head was about to pop, I felt I was being electrocuted.

"I'm dying nurse, I'm fucking dying, please help. Give me more drugs nurse, I need more fucking drugs, gimme loads of fucking drugs."
The drugs weren't reacting fast enough and as the pain increased, I could see death around the corner. All my movements were involuntary and I had no control of my body anymore, I was in survival mode. The young female nurse was visibly shaken and began to cry herself. Now I really did think I was going to die.
"I can't watch this anymore."

As she exited the small room in floods of tears I started talking out loud to myself, I didn't give a fuck who heard me. "What have I done? What have I done to myself? I've killed myself, why the fuck did I do this to myself?" I kept frantically repeating this over and over again, but to no avail. The pain continued. A big male nurse ran in and clocked the fear in my eyes. He immediately rolled me on my side and without warning rammed another capsule up my arse. I took some oral ones too but the drugs were taking too long, it was too late. I was fucked. I passed out temporarily and I thought that was the end. The nurses later told me they thought I wasn't going to survive either, they were watching the last dance of a dead man.

After about 10 minutes I was able to stay still long enough for the female nurse to take my blood pressure. I was still in agony but it was subsiding a little as the beautiful drugs done their job at last. The medics disappeared and I was left with the pain and my own thoughts for another stretch of time, until the nurse came back an hour or so later.

"Your blood pressure was 260/111 Tennyson"

"Is that bad nurse?"

"Yes Tennyson. You went into hypertension 3, I dread to think what your blood pressure was 10 minutes before it was taken. You're lucky to be alive."

"Am I going to die nurse?"

"We don't know exactly what's causing this Tennyson, our specialists believe you may have suffered a burst aneurysm or possibly even a mini stroke."

"Stroke! I'm not even 36 yet nurse, how the fuck am I having strokes?" I was not filled with confidence about my future but I was glad the pain had gone away. I just wanted to sleep now. I was tired, I was so so tired.

Chapter 40

After the specialists had deemed I was in no fit state to go home, I was detained indefinitely until the test results came back. They had no idea I was a chronic alcoholic as I'd lied to protect my drinking. When they asked how much I drank I gave a well practised response.

"No more than a normal person. About 5 on a Friday night and 8-10 on a Saturday." That was bullshit. I knew if I told them the truth they'd blame the booze and tell me to stop drinking. I wasn't ready for death but I wasn't ready for sobriety either.

For three weeks they prodded and poked me with their instruments, trying to figure out while I almost 'popped' like an overheated thermometer. I kept being told I was lucky to be alive. I thought for a second before replying respectfully to a nurse who just helped save my life. "I don't feel lucky nurse. I feel like this is the starter and I've still got the main course to come. I'm afraid." The sympathetic nurse who had just watched a 15 stone, alcoholic, tattooed thug, begging for mercy on the floor, put her hand on my shoulder gently. "You're in the best place now Tennyson, we'll look after you, now try and get some sleep."

During my stay in hospital I ate every meal and drank nothing but water and tea. I was completely alcohol free and even though I was on death's door I actually looked a lot healthier. I hadn't smoked a single cigarette either. The pain had permanently scarred me and I was taking this warning seriously, as long as it didn't involve me quitting the booze. If they had told me the booze had caused this I still wouldn't have stopped, I was too far gone. Numerous blood test were done which all came back clear. I got sent for a CAT scan, then two days later I got sent for another one but this time they ran dye through my blood as well for a clearer image around my brain. I was sent for an ECG to make sure my heart wasn't fucked. The male nurse made me laugh and brightened the mood by telling me I reminded him of Tom Hardy in that voodoo show that was on TV at the time, Taboo.

"Your heart is strong as a bull Tennyson, nothing wrong here."
I'd always been in the habit of calling every medical practitioner I met as 'Doc'. Male or female, I didn't give a fuck, it was Doc. I didn't mean it in a disrespectful way, it was just the way I talked.
"Doc, it's just nice to find out there's a heart in there and not a little black engine fueled by Jack Daniels."
"I've got a feeling you have a hell of a story to tell Tennyson?"
"There's definitely a story there Doc and hell is along for the ride."

The lumber puncture was horrible. It didn't hurt but it just didn't feel natural. I felt sick and dizzy curled up in the fetal position, with a long fucking needle draining fluid from my spine. I started to feel faint and I could feel my blood pressure start to rise as the panic set in and the wave of pain threatened. Thankfully the lumber puncture finished and I fell straight asleep.

So far all the procedures hadn't given anything conclusive and the results were sent to a specialist in another hospital. I was visited a few days later by a neurologist, an Indian gentleman by the name of Mr Aur.
"Where is this man's MRI results nurse?"
"We didn't send him for one Mr Aur."
"Nurse please get the doctor who has been orchestrating this patient's treatment to come and see me at once. I want to know why after three weeks this man still hasn't been sent for an MRI scan? I want Tennyson sent down right now, in front of the queue for the next available scan."
I'd heard horror stories about MRI scans and the claustrophobia, the noise and everything else that made it an uncomfortable place to be. I actually loved it and hadn't felt as relaxed in weeks as I did in that machine.

I was wheeled back to my ward and informed that Mr Aur would get my results in a few days and be back to see me. There would be no more tests until then. During my stay I got to know some of the nurses well. I talked boxing with the two male Filipino nurses on the late shifts, and flirted terribly with the female nurses, regardless of age or looks. It wasn't a sexual thing, just a bit of my character struggling to stay contained in this place.

One night a new female nurse came in from another ward to cover for the night. She had a name tag on but it wasn't hers as she'd left hers at home. I was still a little doped up so I forgot her real name, I've even forgotten the fake name on the tag, but I didn't forget her looks. The nurse was hot. Throughout the evening we laughed and joked quietly and a little sex banter was thrown in. We laughed and held each other's gaze a few seconds too long as the silence came in, the silence you both know means the chemistry is right. I was horny as fuck and would have loved to make a teenage fantasy come true, but it never did. I was left with some great wank bank material however, and considering I hadn't touched my cock for almost a month, other than to piss, I made my way to the disabled toilets to have a stretch thinking about the sexy nurse. I walked down the corridor and locked the large heavy door behind me. I pulled my sweat pants down and sat on the toilet. I'd been thinking about sex for hours so my dick already had a bit of length on the go. It didn't need much revving, a few tugs and I was away, I was away on Porno Island.

After getting about 30 seconds into a month delayed wank I feel the wave of pain go flush across my face. It wasn't the wave of pleasure I was normally used to when I had my cock in my hand, this was the wave of death. I dropped my dick immediately and apart from pissing or showering I didn't touch the fucker for another five weeks. I was devastated that the excitement caused by having a tug had increased my blood pressure to the point of another attack. I kept this new information a secret from the doctors just in case they inform me that not only is my drinking career over but that I'm also no longer aloud to stage the 6 inch Olympics either. Fuck that. These headaches had instilled a fear in me that nothing else in life ever had. I was terrified. The MRI scan came back and Mr Aur informed there had been no burst aneurysms but a mini stroke couldn't be ruled out yet. Mr Aur said they had found shadows on a certain part of my brain but they wouldn't have caused the pain.

"Mr Aur, do you know that means? Mr Gold in Welsh."

"Yes Tennyson I'm aware of that. In Punjabi it actually has its meaning from the phrase 'someone else'."

"Mr Gold and Mr Someone Else! Fucking hell Doc, they are two great names."

Mr Aur had a genuine interest in not only my medical condition but he had suspicions about my drinking and the state of my mental health.

"How much do you drink Tennyson? This is between you and me, it will not go on your records. I want to help you Tennyson but I need you to be honest with me."

Nobody had ever talked to me this way before, until Someone Else turned up. I felt a connection with Mr Aur and I therefore felt obliged to give him more truth than I'd given any other person, I gave him half the story.

"Look Doc. Can I call you Doc, Doc? Anyway Doc, the truth of the matter is I get drunk as fuck every Friday and Saturday night but I'm mostly dry throughout the week."

"Well you're going to have to cut down if you don't want these episodes to return Tennyson."

"Cut down? Fucking hell Doc I only drink 2 days a week, how can I cut down anymore?"

"You're a grown man Tennyson and I can only give you my professional diagnosis. What you then do with that is up to you." I respected that answer.

"Fair enough Doc. Lay it on me straight Doc, no foreplay, just ram it in big boy. Am I going to die?"

Mr Aur went into a speech about my symptoms and the test results and I sort of lost him in all the jargon.

"We have concluded that you are suffering from a rare condition Tennyson. It affects only about 1 in 1000 people, mostly males."

I wasn't listening properly again so immediately jumped to the wrong conclusion.

"Ah for fuck sakes Doc. Is it my cock or balls? What's up with them Doc? Will I be ok?" After exhibiting a look of confusion, then amusement, the Doc shook his head in disbelief and gave a little chuckle.

"You have developed Cluster Headaches Tennyson. These can be brought on by a number of triggers, drinking and smoking being top of the tree. It's mostly seen in men between 20-40 years old."

I'd never heard of this condition before so I pressed the Doc a little more for some information.

"Why are they so painful doc? That was no ordinary headache. Will they come back? Can they be cured? Do I have to stop drinking? Why, when I get a hardon do the headaches start? What the fuck is this all about Doc? Why me?"

"You will have this condition for life Tennyson, there is no cure, only management. You may get them weekly, monthly, yearly, or never again. You may never have one ever again, there is no way of determining sorry Tennyson."

"So basically Doc I'm going to have a deadly, silent assassin, standing over my shoulder for the rest of my life ready to fuck me up if I drink and smoke too much?"

"That's a good analogy Tennyson. Not one I can use in my profession but yes I couldn't really put it any better."

I felt like crying. I was unsure and definitely not confident I would survive another attack. I was told death was uncommon but it was a possibility. I didn't feel like my head was capable of taking another battering and I feared the worst.

"You need to change your lifestyle Tennyson, cut back on the cigarettes and alcohol. Get some light exercise and lose a few pounds and you'll be ok."

"Doc, I seriously considered killing myself on that second attack, I've never done that, and my minds been to some fucked up places Doc. I don't think I can take another episode."

"Funnily enough Tennyson they are actually nicknamed 'suicide headaches', I have known people who have taken their own life over these and I also know people who haven't had an attack for over 20 years."

"Fuck off Doc! Suicide headaches? That's fucked up Doc."

"Yes I am serious Tennyson and yes, it is effed up. How this now progresses is up to you. There is no medical treatment, you just need to be a little kinder to yourself, maybe seek some counselling. Do you live alone Tennyson?"

"Sort of Doc, why you after a piece of ass?"

Another head shake and uncontrolled laughter from Mr Aur before he carried on.

"Hahaha, you're a character Tennyson. Now how often do you drink my friend?"

"Every day Doc."

"That answer needs to change Tennyson."

"I know Doc, I'm sorry for lying."

"Why did you lie Tennyson?"

"Because if I can't drink Doc, I don't want to live, there's no point."

"You're in good shape physically Tennyson. I've read the reports of the episodes, you're a fighter, a tough one too. Certainly tougher than me."

"Yeah and certainly fucking stupider than you as well. Look at me Doc, I've fucking killed myself."

"I see you used to be in the military Tennyson. Do you suffer from PTSD?"

"PTSD? Does that's stand for Pissed on a Saturday?"

"No Tennyson, it stands for Post Traumatic Stress Disorder. Many military personal end up suffering from this."

"No doc, I'm good on that. I was a massive fucking idiot even before I joined the Navy, I can't lay the blame at their door for this."

"Well my friend you will suffer from it now. You've had a life changing experience Tennyson, you will never look at life in the same way again.

Women who have suffered from cluster headaches claim the pain is much worse than childbirth."

"I've never felt a pain like it Doc."

"Hopefully you won't again Tennyson but it's in your hands now. Change your lifestyle, stop drinking, and any drugs that are not prescribed, stop taking them."

"Ok Doc."

"Read up on PTSD Tennyson, I think it will be of benefit to you. Read up on alcoholism as well, you don't have to feel ashamed."

"I will Doc, thanks man."

"That's ok Tennyson, do you have any other questions for me before I leave?"

"If I don't stop drinking doc will I die?"

"You will soon be turning 36 Tennyson. If you carry on your lifestyle of drinking and drugs you will be the best looking corpse in South Wales before your 40th birthday."

"I hear you Doc, thanks for the honesty."

Mr Aur started to pack up his things as we engaged in a bit of small talk. He got up to leave and put his hand on my shoulder as he could see I was heartbroken at the news. I now had to contemplate divorcing my life long liquid partner. I was devastated. The drugs I could take or leave, didn't give a fuck. But alcohol was my life blood. The Doc dropped some lyrics on me before he left.

"Knowledge is knowing a tomato is a fruit. Wisdom is knowing not to put it in a fruit salad. You have the tools Tennyson, you just don't have the wisdom yet to know what tools you need to use for each job, but you're smarter than you give yourself credit for, you'll figure it out. If you want to."

"I don't know about that Doc, look where I am."

"You're alive Tennyson, that's where you are, that's all you need right now. Open your mind, there are physical illnesses and mental illnesses. Physically you're in great shape, mentally not so much. Look into

meditation and spirituality Tennyson, I think it will help you. You need to find yourself."
"Some hippy shit Doc? I'm down for that. Thanks a lot man."
And with that Mr Aur picked up his black satchel and began to leave, "Take care Tennyson, I hope I don't see you in my workplace again."

"Me neither Doc, me neither."

Chapter 41

Three days later I was discharged from hospital and sent home. There was nothing further that could be done. It was down to me now. I was prescribed a strip of 30mg Dihydrocodiene pills, the strong fuckers. I was told by the nurse before I left. "If you have another episode Tennyson, take one pill and lie in a dark room until the symptoms go away."

I was then told if the pain was not going after one hour just to call 999. These pills were strong and highly addictive, probably not the best thing to give an alcoholic, but apart from Mr Aur, nobody was aware of my alcoholism. I put the pills in a drawer and I didn't think about them for over a year. Then one evening in an alcohol fused madness I dropped all fifteen and overdosed. Survived again but I still wasn't getting my head around this spirituality shit Mr Aur had told me about.

I'd been off work for a month and the hospital gave me another paper, signing me off for another three weeks to recover. More than one hospital employee had told me that staring at a monitor for 8 hours a day for 12 years wasn't the best way to avoid further attacks either. Stress was a major trigger just like booze and drugs.

For the next three weeks I sat at home listening to music and watching movies. I'd go for long walks to get a little exercise and I ate and drank well. I still hadn't touched the booze. This stress free way of living appealed to me and I quickly removed myself from social media as well. For large parts of the day, I would leave my phone in a different room. As I wasn't on my phone much it meant I wasn't chasing women on dating sites either. I didn't even stretch my cock until the night before I went back to work. It was a great tug, better than ever, it felt like I'd popped my cherry again. For the first time in years, I felt like a free man. I was positive and well nourished, strong and as healthy as I could hope for in the circumstances.

I returned to work the next day and I was back on the booze as soon as my shift ended. All the good work I'd put in was flushed down the fucking toilet as I hit the old, reliable button all alkies have, the 'fuck it' button. The beast was back.

Within two weeks I was drinking more than ever and if I wasn't suicidal, which I claimed, then I sure had a strange way of showing it. At least there was a bit of good news while I was in hospital and it made me think maybe we all get what's coming to us. Karma's a bitch and if you fuck her over one too many times, she will eventually fuck you back, harder!

Chapter 42

The office looked the same but I was viewing it now as a different person. Even though I had fallen off the wagon after my first day back in work. I could definitely feel I had changed. Maybe for the worse. How many more times could I cheat death? I didn't have too many fights left in me. I was tired and my 40th birthday was just a few short years away.

One of the new girls on the team, Clarissa, offered to let me sit next to her on my first day back. It would be beneficial to see calls being taken and the system used again as I'd been away for two months.

Clarissa was a young girl and she went into a detailed story that shocked me, sickened me, but ultimately made me happy.

"Ok Ten, do you know Jerome?"

"He's our fucking boss Clarissa, of course I know him."

"Ok, so you know he was having an affair with Jacqui right?"

"Yeah."

"And you know he's married to Starr right?"

"Fucking hell Clarissa, I know all this, let's get the juicy shit."

"Ok, ok, ok, give me a minute Ten."

Clarissa settled herself and then took a quick look around to see if she could be overheard, before going into detail.

"Well, Starr moved out of the house, packed all her stuff and left. She made a few trips back and forth to collect all her stuff while Jerome wasn't there."

"That's good Clarissa, I didn't know any of this so please continue. You want a coffee? Hold on, let me get some coffees."

When I got back from the machine with two shitty flat white coffees, I handed one to Clarissa, who couldn't wait to give me a detailed account of what had happened. I couldn't believe it but then I thought about what a cunt Jerome was and suddenly I wasn't surprised.

Jerome had travelled to work one morning and given Starr permission to enter her own house, to remove her own belongings. Starr didn't want to make any more trips than were required so took as much as she could. Weirdly she also wanted to leave the house tidy so gave it a full clean, leaving it spotless before she departed for the final time.

As Starr was cleaning the bottom of the wardrobe, she found a little opening with a false wall covering it, no more than the size of a shoe box.

"Fucking hell, the dirty fucker got even more poor women on the go?"
"Hold on Ten, let me tell the story."
"Ok, ok, carry on."
"So…."

Clarissa went on to explain that in the opening Starr had found some letters and cards. Initially she couldn't determine what the letters were about as the language used was so childlike. The letters turned out to be from Jacqui to Jerome, sexually explicit letters detailing what they had been up to, nothing was held back in the naïve writings. Jacqui wrote about how she loved Jerome and he was the only man for her, all the usual soppy bullshit. Starr wished to herself that she hadn't read the letters and in a fit of frustration tore one up.

The ripped up letter she left on the floor as a final 'fuck you' to Jerome, even though she knew he wouldn't care. The other letters she left in the envelope she found, thinking she knew the full story, when in fact she knew fuck all. The ripped up letter on the floor from Jacqui had a date on one of the torn bits of paper. The letter was dated 9 years ago, and Jacqui was only 22 right now. It turned out that Jerome had been grooming Jacqui since before she was a teenager, and then forced her into a sexual relationship when she turned 13. Starr was even more distraught about this than all the other stuff that had gone on, it broke her. She took all the letters and went to the police station.

During the subsequent police interviews and investigations, it turned out that Jacqui was unaware there was a legal age of consent. Jerome had told her that as long as she was with an adult it didn't matter. Jerome had fed her lies and manipulated for years, Jacqui was unaware that her knight in shining armour was actually a fucking pedophile and she was his victim.

The police turned up at the call centre and arrested Jerome in work, in front of all the staff. In the court case a few months down the line a judge would say Jerome was a narcissist of the highest order, a control freak and a dangerous pedophile. It turns out that Jacqui wasn't his only victim. Jerome was found guilty and sentenced to 9 years in jail. The last thing I will say about that fucking kiddie fiddler, is that I regret the old team weren't there to see him carted off by the police. I was in hospital. Sharkhead, Glug, Jess, Mario, Pacman, Sadie, Karley, were all gone. One positive came out of it. Starr was told what Glug said to Jerome before he got sacked for getting his cock out. She made the approach to Glug once Jerome got sent down and they ended up staying local and going into business together. They suited each other. I was an old head in a young person's job. All my friends were gone, I had nobody I could trust, and I had nobody in my life. I had the drugs and alcohol. And I had the misery, I always had the misery.

Chapter 43

Recently the four voices of the apocalypse had been talking to me more. We'd get back into the old habits of arguing like a bunch of pissed up sailors on shore leave. We had some good times but Dev, Ref and Gel were sad. They could tell I wasn't happy anymore and as usual, Dev was the first to open my mouth.

"Shall we fuck off Ten? Do you want us to go? We're hurting you Ten."
I started to cry as I told Dev, Ref and Gel not to leave me, they were all I had in this world, they were the only people I trusted and they weren't even real. I'd tried to stop drinking numerous times, but I couldn't. I'd

resigned myself to the fact that I was an alcoholic, this was my life. I was born to drink myself to death.

Even though I was drinking more than ever I was still training too. I'd started boxing again on a heavy bag I'd put up in my shed. It felt good to be slamming the bag, taking out all my frustrations on an inanimate object.

One afternoon while half cut, I was punching fuck out of the bag when I got what I can only describe now as a sign. Maybe a blessing, but it felt like the realist thing I'd ever experienced. Was this spirituality?
Earlier in the day I'd downloaded the Bob Marley album, 'Catch a Fire.' I'd owned this album on CD since the 1990s, however, unbeknown to me at the time, I'd downloaded the deluxe reissued version with added tracks.
As I hit fuck out of the bag with my 14oz gloves my life once again changed. A higher power spoke to me for the first time. Words I'd never heard before.

'In high seas or in low seas,
I'm gonna be your friend
I'm gonna be your friend.
In high seas or in low seas,
I'll be by your side
I'll be by your side.'

As the words soaked into my mind all my technique disappeared. I hit the punch bag with animalistic ferocity. A feral fury erupted from my soul, as I emptied everything I had bottled up through my fists.
The shed was shaking and so was I. The tears rolled down my face as I had a full mental breakdown right there. I cried and punched in a manic fury, I wanted to kill the world for what I perceived as it's personal grudge against me. Apart from the voices in my head, the only true

friend I felt I had was a Jamaican musician who had been dead for 35 years. My mask of sanity was slipping and I knew I was truly alone. It was death or redemption for me, and no in between. Bob's words and voice triggered a feeling like no other, it was like he was talking directly to me. A song I'd never heard before containing the words and support I needed at that exact time. It was spooky. Before the song had ended. I was on my knees, crying and exhausted while letting out a blood curdling scream from the depths of my damaged soul. Even though I didn't quit drinking that day, I'd gained something more, I'd gained a higher power. I wouldn't know how to use this yet but I remembered Mr Aur's words about wisdom and knowledge. All in good time.

I was getting older and I was lonely. I was an alcoholic and a drug addict. Over the years I had admitted these two things numerous times, however, I'd never accepted it. I'd never accepted that I was powerless over alcohol and I thought could quit when I wanted. I couldn't, I tried, and failed. It was time to accept the fact I was an alcoholic and I made the decision I wasn't ready to quit yet. There were still a few more floors to explore before I finally hit my rock bottom.

I walked to work the next day, over dog shit bridge and then down the river path, I was still thinking about my experience in the shed the day before. This rollercoaster of destiny, or maybe it's a rollercoaster of fate, was still going through the loop da loops. I didn't realise until years later that it was actually a rollercoaster of choice. I could have got off whenever I wanted, but the sickness in my head made me carry on ride that fucker. I would eventually hit rock bottom and go out in a blaze of broken dreams and a wasted life. But, to be where I am now, maybe meant I needed to stay here a little longer. I'm not saying my dark times are any darker than yours, I'm just saying only I have been through my dark times and only you have been through yours.

For the time being (well for the next 22 months) before I find my serenity, I'll continue living my life in a thunderstorm.

May 11th 2016

6 months

12 months

22 months

March 3rd 2018

Text Message:

He got 18 years and you have a son. I've been watching you babe, you're not well. We're going to get you into rehab. I kept the key you gave me as my only reminder of you. My one true love. Thank you for not changing the locks. Hurry home because your dog Kano is here, you must have locked him out. We love you xxx

Genevieve

Recovery

Rebirth

Redemption

Serenity

For another time......

THE END

The Soundtrack

It took me three months to break the back of this story. I'd like to thank the following artists and the albums they produced for getting the story out of my head and onto paper.

Outkast – Southernplayalisticadillacmuzik
Screaming Trees – Sweet Oblivion
Poppa LQ – Your Entertainment, My Reality
Benny the Butcher – Burden of Proof
Ghetts – Conflict of Interest
Fredo – Money Can't Buy Happiness
Portishead – Dummy
Sleaford Mods – All That Glue
Ransom – Directors Cut ep (1,2,3)
Mark Lanegan – Whiskey for the Holy Ghost
Spice 1 – 187 He Wrote
Will Wood – The Normal Album (thanks Teagan xxx)
Marlon Craft – Funhouse Mirror
Freddie Gibbs – Bandana & Alfredo
Nas – Kings Disease
Above the Law – Uncle Sam's Curse
DMX – All Albums

Tupac and Bob Marley everyday